D0852715

To Rima, the Queen of my kingdom
ADL

For Carolyn, who makes me able
MPM

JSharp

The Lone and Level Sands

A. David Lewis

mpMann

& Jennifer Rodgers

Second (color) Edition published by
ASP Comics LLC
96 Linwood Plaza PMB 360
Fort Lee, NJ 07024-3701

www.aspcomics.com

Original Caption Box edition
ISBN 0-9765811-0-8
ASP Comics LLC edition
ISBN 1-932386-12-2

SECOND EDITION, December 2005
0 9 8 7 6 5 4 3 2 1

Printed in China.

FOREWORD

"To the victor, the spoils" goes the old saying, conjuring images of triumphant troops returning home bearing chests filled with the gold and jewels of their vanquished foes. Yet, like Percy Shelley's"Ozymandias" referenced in the title of this book you now hold in your hands), gold, jewels and the empires they fuel have a tendency to fade in time; and like now-humble salt, which for periods was so valuable that it served as currency, what was once saught-after plunder can become negligible in time. Is there then truly nothing but ephemera to fill the coffers of the victorious? Certainly not; there is another old saying which, while not as old, is perhaps more insightful: "The winners write the history books."

I'm not sure exactly when in elementary school one first begins studying U.S. history, but I remember being quite young when I first began to learn about the Civil War. I grew up in southeastern Virginia, and I recall coming home from school and asking my mother,"What side did we fight on in the Civil War?" She explained to me that Virginia was part of the Confederacy and Richmond its capitol.

"So we were the bad guys?" I asked, disappointed.

My mother explained to me, as best she could to a child, I imagine, that complex conflicts don't often break down into easy classifications--into the victorious "good guys' and rightly defeated "bad guys."

It's easy to write off a young child's equation of Winners = "good guys"/ Losers = "bad guys" as understandable naiveté, perhaps in this case augmented by an unhealthy diet of sci-fi movies and superhero comic books. History shows, though, that this formula isn't confined to childhood gaffs and genre fiction. U.S. General Curtis LeMay's comment on the firebombing of sixty-seven Japanese cities during World War II, part of a tactical strategy he helped develop, is a case in point: "If [we] had lost the war, I would have been tried as a war criminal." It's a trenchant comment, unsettling not simply because of the events to which it refers, but also because its brutal honesty calls into question the shared narrative of our history-- a history shaped largely by conflict and often couched in the all-too-comfortable terms of good vs. bad and right vs. wrong.

Anyone raised in the Judeo-Christian tradition shared by much of the Western World has likely heard at least the Sunday School version of Exodus: The noble Moses, with the help of the one true God, who unleashes a series ofamazing plagues, leads his people, the Israelites, to freedom from the oppressive yoke of the cruel Egyptians. Even this version of the story, though, doesn't do justice to the source text, which is often interpreted through the filter of the later books of the New Testament. Like much of the Old Testament, Exodus is a tale rife with brutal violence, searing conflict and an often wrathful Deity whose modus operandi is more, "An eye for an eye, a tooth for a tooth" than "Turn the other cheek."

The Israelites were in fact slaves of the Egyptian monarchy, and slavery is a practice without moral defense. Yet, one need not descend into the murky depths of moral relativism to posit that there is in fact more than one perspective from which to view the events of Exodus-- to understand that all human conflict is in fact human and as such is a conflict between individuals like ourselves with goals, feelings, interests and motivations not entirely unlike our own. We take odd comfort of the cliché of the dastardly villain with the handlebar moustache who does evil for evil's sake precisely because we know no such entity exists in the real world. It is often only through the lens of history that what is right and what is wrong becomes codified. In the near view, all of us simply seek to do what we each believe to be most right-- to act otherwise is not to act as a true human acts.

This then is what drives A. David Lewis and mpMann's ***The Lone and Level Sands***: not the trite modernist trope of a simple switch of narrative perspective (Cinderella through the eyes of the Wicked Step-Sister, etc.) but rather the story of Exodus cast not as parable but as human drama-- a powerful struggle between real human characters with all-too-human ambitions, conflicts and flaws.

In ***The Lone and Level Sands*** we see Moses not only as the instrument of his people's freedom, but also as the arrogant agent of a powerful and wrathful deity. "Where is your nation now?" he asks, taunting Ramses as Yahweh's plague of locusts devours the dwindling food supply of the Pharaoh's people.

The Ramses of ***Sands*** is not a straw man slave master, but a conflicted monarch who's inherited a conflict not of his making, and who's become an unwitting cog ground down in a divine clockwork. While we, of course, rejoice in the well-known and inevitable conclusion to this narrative of the oppressed-- that is, freedom from the oppressor.

The Lone and Level Sands brings a depth and empathetic quality to the story's characters that defies the unambiguous good vs. evil distinctions of exodus' more didactic tellings. Again, Percy Shelley: "In a drama of the highest order there is little food for censure and hatred; it teaches rather self-knowledge and self-respect.

Enjoy.

-Ben Towle

INTRODUCTION

One of the most attractive challenges to doing ***The Lone and Level Sands*** was in meshing together the various sources. I wanted to take the biblical sources as fact, but also as non-religious; I wanted to take the anthropological sources equally as fact, but without favoring them over the events in Exodus. Finally, there were further elements like the Qur'an and the modern ***Ten Commandments*** film that I also wanted to incorporate.

The best passages in the book are those that manage to be the most amalgamated and synthesized. The story is told "on the ground" focusing on the human reaction of the Egyptians to fear and hate their once-powerless slaves. This is where the Bible leaves the most gaps to be filled. Without taking too many liberties, I tried to seize upon those vacancies in Exodus, particularly on the human reactions of Ramses, Moses and their respective people.

Marv and I had to inject the "humanity" into scenes that are told so starkly and even enigmatically in the Old Testament. Finding a true role for Aaron was terrific. He becomes a rich character, half well-spoken diplomat, half prodding malcontent. After a life of enslavement, he's more pointed than Moses, yet less connected to the divine source. As a Levite priest, he aches to enact his brother's prophecies and commands. Moses is more conflicted, with close connections to the Egyptian royal family as well as to his God. Coming directly from his visions, his convoluted speech gives Aaron a better role as his spokesperson.

But, really, Ramses is the main character of ***The Lone and Level Sands***. Somewhere between Percy Blysshe Shelley's ***Ozymandias*** and Exodus lay his story. Whether he is known as *The Son of Ra*, *Ramses the Great*, *Ozymandias*, or the evil *Pharaoh* of the Israelites, the truth of his life may forever remain a mystery, closed from the light of scientific anthropology and archeology...

...but not from speculation and creative thought. In fact, such an enigma is positively alluring to the storytelling mind. Between the evil of the Exodus-Pharaoh and the majesty of the New Kingdom's deliverer, there emerges the man of our story: a father, a statesman, a firebrand, a lover, a monarch, and a mortal. How interesting, then, to tell his story (or one of his possible stories) reflected back through the prisms of Exodus, the Qur'an, and the Torah's *Shermat*.

Unlike many previous accounts, I believe, ***The Lone and Level Sands'*** Ramses is a very dynamic character: he grows and suffers and changes by the end of the story. Our book is not meant to let him off the hook, per se: there was almost certainly slavery, which he permitted; he continually revoked his promises to the Israelites, and so forth. But instead of easily vilifying him, we explore him further – and Moses and Aaron and the rest of the cast – as more of a human being who may have done wrong (either willingly or by destiny) rather than as a legendary evil or faultless king. I hope that Marv and I have managed to explore all of the characters that way-- as humans-- imbuing an epic story with that additional layer of intrigue.

-ADL

THE LONE AND LEVEL SANDS

THE LONE & LEVEL SANDS

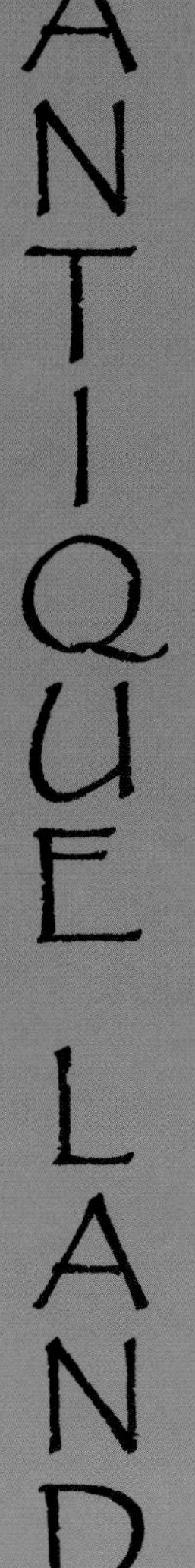

~Year 14~
of Egypt's Nineteenth Dynasty,
in the Reign of Seti I.

THEY'VE RETURNED!
ALERT THE QUEEN--
"--THEY'RE BACK!"
"THE PHARAOH HAS RETURNED!"

MY KING.
GOOD AND TRUSTED CO-REGENT-- HOW FARES MY KINGDOM?

GREAT PHARAOH SETI, IT *FLOURISHES* NOW BY AMON-RA'S GRACE TO HAVE YOU SAFELY RETURNED FROM HITTITE BATTLE TO TANNIS, WHERE--
CO-REGENT... MY STOMACH IS FULL OF BATTLE AND BLOOD, THE MOST SADLY UNCIVILIZED OF MAN'S MANUFACTURES. THE STAINED FLAG OF VICTORY RETURNS ME TO THE BELOVED BOSOM OF EGYPT--

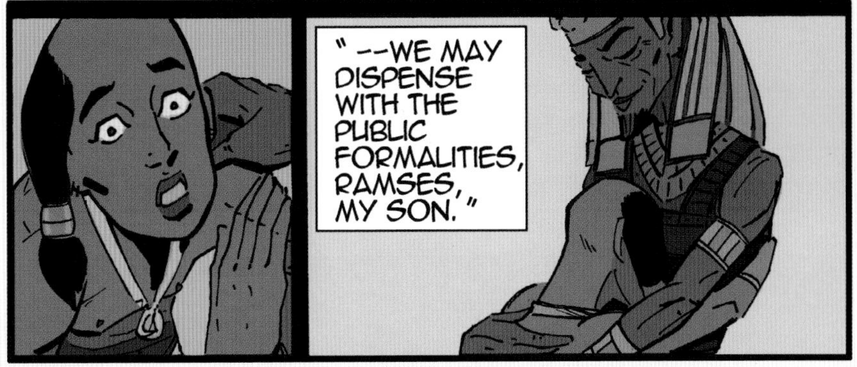
" --WE MAY DISPENSE WITH THE PUBLIC FORMALITIES, RAMSES, MY SON."

THAT EVENING...

FATHER?
OOPS, PARDON ME, MOSES.
MMM... UH, YES... CERTAINLY...

--AH! HERE MY BOY-KING IS NOW. I WAS JUST TELLING YOUR MOTHER THAT WE PASSED KARNAK ON OUR WAY HOME.
YES, YES, FATHER.
SOMEDAY SON, YOU MAY COMPLETE THAT WHICH *YOUR* FATHER HAS BEGUN--
YES MOTHER, BUT--
--PHARAOH, THERE ARE STILL... *MATTERS* TO DISCUSS.

IS THERE SOMETHING SERIOUS THE MATTER, RAMSES?
OH, I'M SURE MY LITTLE APRICOT JUST NEEDS TIME TO DISCUSS A FEW OF THE NEW RECONSECRATIONS, TUY... WE'LL BE BACK SHORTLY.
I AM RELIEVED THAT YOU ARE FINALLY EXPRESSING TO YOUR FATHER THIS ...
...CONCERN ABOUT YOUR COUSIN--
TA. WE FOLLOW WHAT PATHS ARE WRITTEN FOR US-- AND CERTAINLY, YOU ARE A WELL AND TRUSTED FRIEND OF MY SON. BUT I WOULD NOT HAVE YOU GOSSIP ABOUT THE ROYAL FAMILY ALOUD.
O-OF... OF COURSE, SIRE...
BUT THE PROBLEM IS A ROYAL, FATHER--
--IT'S MOSES.

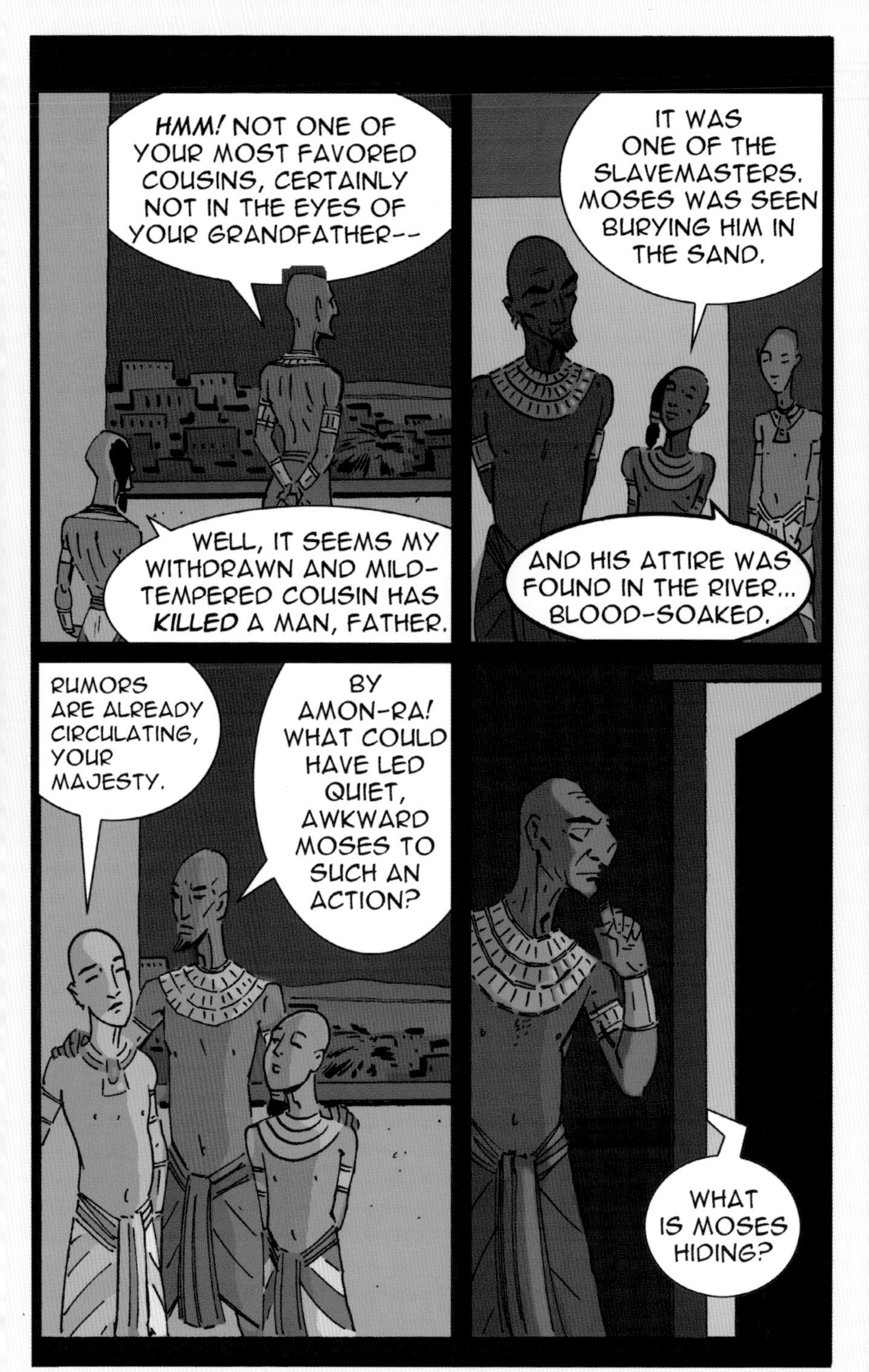

HMM! NOT ONE OF YOUR MOST FAVORED COUSINS, CERTAINLY NOT IN THE EYES OF YOUR GRANDFATHER--
WELL, IT SEEMS MY WITHDRAWN AND MILD-TEMPERED COUSIN HAS KILLED A MAN, FATHER.
IT WAS ONE OF THE SLAVEMASTERS. MOSES WAS SEEN BURYING HIM IN THE SAND.
AND HIS ATTIRE WAS FOUND IN THE RIVER... BLOOD-SOAKED.
RUMORS ARE ALREADY CIRCULATING, YOUR MAJESTY.
BY AMON-RA! WHAT COULD HAVE LED QUIET, AWKWARD MOSES TO SUCH AN ACTION?
WHAT IS MOSES HIDING?

Later...

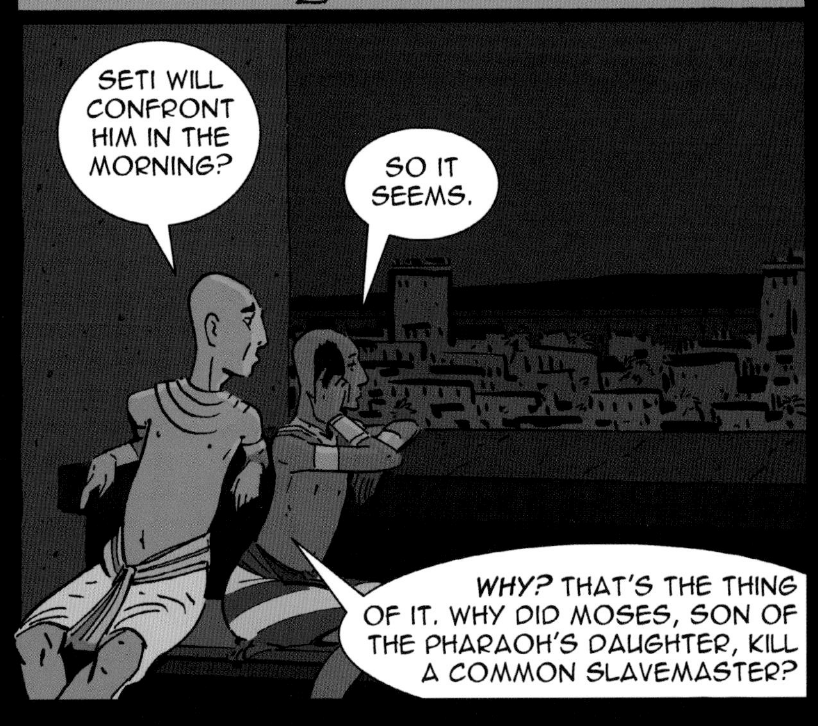

SETI WILL CONFRONT HIM IN THE MORNING?
SO IT SEEMS.
WHY? THAT'S THE THING OF IT. WHY DID MOSES, SON OF THE PHARAOH'S DAUGHTER, KILL A COMMON SLAVEMASTER?

"HMMMMM... **YES.** WHY KILL A SLAVEMASTER?"

"UNLESS YOU WERE A SLAVE."

"MMM... WELL, YES, I SUPPOSE."

"--UNLESS YOU WERE A SLAVE--"

Seti died five years later. Tuy gave the crown directly to her son-- she died ten years after Ramses was named Pharaoh. Moses was never captured. And he never saw Tannis again.

Canto One

"I love my kingdom, my Egypt."
"I love this place, Abu Simbel."

"I was brought to this site as a child, when my uncle ordained construction begun here. I had never been so far from home."
"I came with the royals, with the builders and their slaves. But others soon joined us."
"*Abu Simbel* soon teemed with merchants and traders, fishermen and bakers, priests and heathens. Even other children."
"It grew as I grew, rich in *Amon-Ra's* love."
"Upon his death, my uncle's *crown* passed to his son. The new lord made sure the site--now a city--would not *perish* with his sire."

"I love its soft sands. Its sturdy rock. Its sounds of the *living*. But above all else, I love its *king*. My *pharaoh*. My *husband*— *Ramses*."

NEFERTARI...
You have been out here much of the morning...
THINKING...
SO MUCH IS MINE TO COMMAND, YET... I WOULD HAVE IT THAT MY FATHER HAD LIVED TO SEE THIS LAND SO NEAR TO COMPLETION.
He saw it, husband, in his mind's eye. And he knew it was your destiny to complete Abu Simbel.
HMMM... PERHAPS.
Great Amon-Ra made this your accomplishment, my love. A gift to your people that shall be known for all time.

"Look upon your works, mighty Pharaoh... and *rejoice*!"

--SUCH AS THE BATTLE OF KADESH, WHICH IS ALREADY BEING TAUGHT AS A TEST OF THE YOUNG CO-REGENT'S TENACITY, RATHER THAN AS A VICTORY AGAINST THE "EVIL HITTITES."
HMMP!
PHARAOH RAMSES AND I TEETHED TOGETHER IN SETI'S COURT. I KNOW HE HAS NO GREATER PRIORITY THAN THE PEACE TREATY WITH YOUR HITTITE PEOPLE.
THE AMORITES AND JEBUSITES GATHER AT OUR BORDERS, VIZIER TA.
TRUE, THEY ARE NOT EGYPTIANS, BUT THEY ARE FORMIDABLE.
AND WHERE WILL THE EGYPTIAN ARMY BE WHEN OUR LANDS ARE BESIEGED?
I WILL TELL YOU--
--IF MY CHIEF COUNSELOR, TA, WILL YIELD ME THE FLOOR...?
PHARAOH! YOU GRACE THESE TALKS WITH YOUR DIVINE PRESENCE. HAIL, SON OF RA!

HITTITE AMBASSADOR-- YOUR NAME...?
ANITTAS.
ANITTAS, YOU ASK WHERE WE WILL BE IF YOU ARE ASSAILED?
YES, PHARAOH.
THE TREATY SAYS THAT EITHER NATION CAN CALL ON THE OTHER IN TIME OF WAR. THEREFORE, IF AMON-RA SMILES, WE SHALL BE MARCHING WITH YOU IN THE PARADE OF VICTORY.
"AND IF YOUR GOD DOES NOT SMILE, PHARAOH?"
"THEN WE WILL BLEED WITH YOU IN THE SAND, AMBASSADOR."

PHARAOH, WILL YOU PERMIT ME TO SPEAK FREELY, AS PERHAPS A FRIEND?
I WOULD LIKE THAT, ANITTAS.
WE HOPE YOU WILL ENJOY THE ACCOMODATIONS BEFORE YOUR DEPARTURE.
I MET YOUR FATHER, LONG AGO. A STRONG MAN. A GOOD KING. AND A NOBLE LEADER--
--BUT FOR ALL OF HIS GRACES, I MUST SAY THAT MY TIME WITH YOU TODAY AS EGYPT'S SOVERIEGN HAS PROVEN THE PHARAOH SETI AN ASS NEXT TO YOUR OWN MAJESTY.
WELL THEN, FOR MY FATHER I CURSE YOU AND YOUR PROGENY, BUT FOR MYSELF I THANK YOU FROM THE BOTTOM OF MY HEART. MAY YOU HAVE A PEACEFUL AND SPEEDY RETURN TO ALEPPO.

YOU LIKE HIM.
OH, I WORSHIP HIM. OF COURSE, HE WAS NOT AS ENDEARING UNTIL YOU ARRIVED.
BUT YOU MANAGED TO KEEP THE PEACE... WHILE NEFERTARI AND I ENJOYED A PRIVATE MORNING.
"AND YOU'RE WELCOME. INCIDENTLY. RAMSES... CONCERNING YOUR FATHER--"
WAIT.
WAS I DUE TO MEET WITH THE FARMING MINISTER?

BEFORE YOU MET WITH NEFERTARI, YES. GO, GO!
THERE WAS SOMETHING YOU WANTED TO--?
LATER. WE CAN TALK DOWN IN THE PARLOR LATER-- NOW. GO!

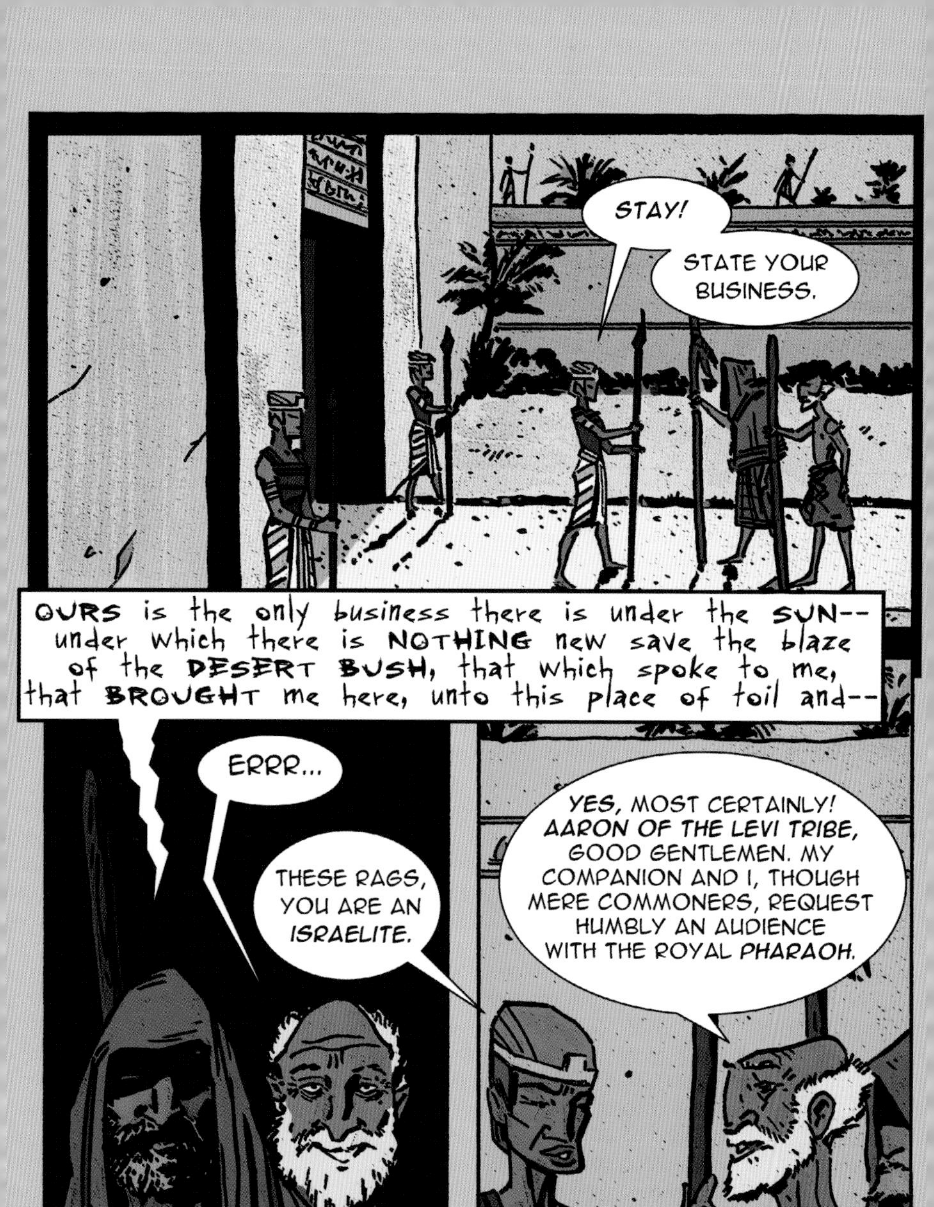
STAY!
STATE YOUR BUSINESS.
OURS is the only business there is under the SUN-- under which there is NOTHING new save the blaze of the DESERT BUSH, that which spoke to me, that BROUGHT me here, unto this place of toil and--
ERRR...
THESE RAGS, YOU ARE AN ISRAELITE.
YES, MOST CERTAINLY! AARON OF THE LEVI TRIBE, GOOD GENTLEMEN. MY COMPANION AND I, THOUGH MERE COMMONERS, REQUEST HUMBLY AN AUDIENCE WITH THE ROYAL PHARAOH.
HAH! THE PHARAOH WOULD NEVER WASTE HIS TIME WITH SUCH TRASH!

...THEN PERHAPS YOU COULD DELIVER THIS MESSAGE ON OUR BEHALF...
"While nowhere near as grand as the main parlor of the Avaris palace, the activity within the Abu Simbel residence warms my heart."

"Here, the Pharaoh's wives take the opportunity to socialize with each other. Their children play together as kindred half-siblings."
"And the officers of the court can once again be part of a community and forget their responsibilities."
"Or try to."

THE MINISTER TOLD YOU ALREADY, I EXPECT. TWO MONTHS. OUR HARVEST STOCKS WILL FALL SHORT OF THE NEXT CYCLE BY TWO MONTHS.
...DO WE RESORT TO...
I AM WATCHING THE GAME, SON OF RA.
"GRANDFATHER! I AM WINNING AGAINST FATHER!"
THE GAME BEARS YOUR NAME, SETI. EVEN AS A BOY, KHEPSESHEF WAS NEVER VERY GOOD AT--
ramses.
I AM NOT ACCUSTOMED TO BEING INTERRUPTED TWICE IN AS MANY MOMENTS...
two israelites at the entrance seek an audience, ramses.
ARE THERE NOW. AND TELL ME, WISE GUARDSMAN, WHY SHOULD I SEE THEM?
"i bear a message from him, ramses."
OH?
"does your father still watch you sleep, little apricot?"

..AN ISRAELITE SAID THIS?
...NNH... I'M SORRY, SIRE...?
THE ISRAELITES... I... I WILL SEE THEM.
"YOU WILL?"

YES, YES. WHY NOT? I AM CERTAINLY... INTRIGUED.
THEN I WILL JOIN YOU--
NO, TA...
I'M SURE IT IS NOTHING.
"LITTLE APRICOT"-- IT IS WHAT YOU CALL ME, FATHER.
"AND WHAT YOUR GRANDFATHER CALLED ME, SETI."

"They are calling it the New Kingdom."

"The dynasty that Ramses' grandfather began--
the one which our son will one day continue..."
"As will his son, darling Seti."
"Historians have already begun to mark this time of greatness with that title: The New Kingdom."
...HMN?
"And while it is a pleasant time, it leaves me with a fear."

"For nothing can remain new forever."

TA, WHAT IS THE COMMOTION?
I ONLY KNOW THAT YOUR FATHER CALLED FOR THESE FOREMEN.
THE REST WE LEARN TOGETHER.

"How long can our time endure?"

"SUMMON BEKENKHONSU."

IT'S BEEN TWO DAYS, AARON! HOW LONG CAN OUR PEOPLE KEEP UP THIS TOIL? NOT JUST *BUILDING* THE TEMPLE, BUT OBTAINING THE *BRICKS* AS WELL!
I KNOW, ELDER, I KNOW...
... NO DOUBT PHARAOH *ORDERED* THIS AGAINST THE ISRAELITES IN RESPONSE TO OUR VISIT.

BAH, "FOREMEN"-- *SLAVEMASTERS*, THEY ARE!
REGARDLESS, THIS WAS ALL *FORESEEN*.
HMMP! JUST AS WITH YOUR PREDICTION THAT THE EGYPTIANS WILL *HAND US* THEIR WEALTH, AARON.
I SAW NO SUCH THING, ELDER--

IT WAS MY *BROTHER*.
MOSES.
THE *RAGGED* FOOL WHO FORESAW YOU *RESIST* OUR ADVICE AND SEND YOUR *SUPERVISORS* TO RAMSES.
MAY THEY GO WITH GOD--

"--SINCE **HE** CERTAINLY DOES NOT GO WITH THEM."

"TIME MEANS NOTHING."

IT IS NOT ONLY UNJUST, SETH-- IT IS LUNACY! HOW CAN PHARAOH LISTEN AND JUST TURN US AWAY WHEN WE HAVE COME TO SAVE HIS OWN WORKFORCE??

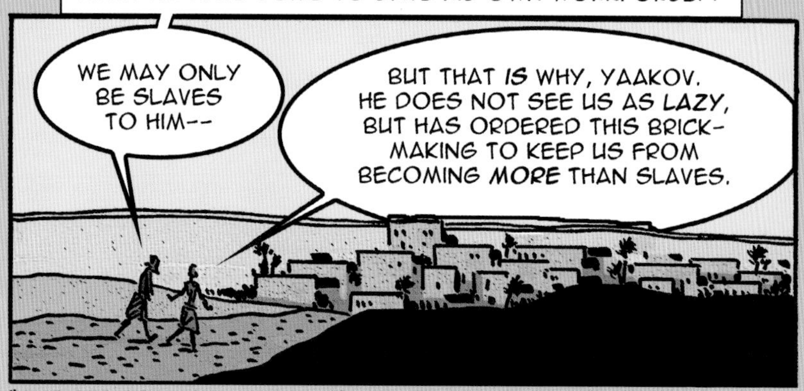

"BUT THE TOIL IS KILLING US! WE ARE THE APPOINTED SUPERVISORS, SETH. WE MUST CONVINCE PHARAOH TO LESSON HIS DEMANDS!"

"Bekenkhonsu had been Ramses' spiritual advisor ever since my husband was a child. Following their quite short meeting with the Israelite supervisors, Bekenkhonsu advised Ramses to relax with his family."

"Khepseshef had already left with Ta to prepare the main palace, but both Seti and I had stayed and waited over *two days* for Ramses to emerge from his urgent business."

"We were both delighted when he took Bekenkhonsu's advice and finally did rejoin us."

You have *finally* stopped frowning.

MMM. YOUR HANDS ARE ALMOST AS SOOTHING AS YOUR LAP, MY QUEEN.

THE HITTITES, CROP CONCERNS, THE TEMPLE CONSTRUCTION... THEY **ALL** WEIGH ON MY MIND.

"BUT OF ALL THESE WORRIES, IT IS THE ISRAELITES WHO MOST TROUBLE ME WITH THEIR CRAZED QUEST... THEIR STRANGE FAITH..."

No doubt your heart bleeds even for the slaves. You have no love for the edict your grandfather set upon them.

YES, NO DOUBT...

MY WISE AND LOVELY CONSORT.

Wise and concerned. I have seen you dwell on this before. Perhaps you will address this issue in Avaris.

YES, I PLANNED--

RETURN TO AVARIS? GRANDFATHER, WILL WE STILL HAVE TIME TO SWIM?

HA! WHY, YES, SETI MY WATERBUG. WE STILL HAVE A FEW DAYS LEFT HERE ALONG THE WATERS.

"I think you should have been named *drawn from the water,* little apricot."

MORE APPROPRIATE THAN YOU KNOW MY LADY...

"Bekenkhonsu?"

"MY LORD RAMSES... THEY HAVE ***RETURNED...***"

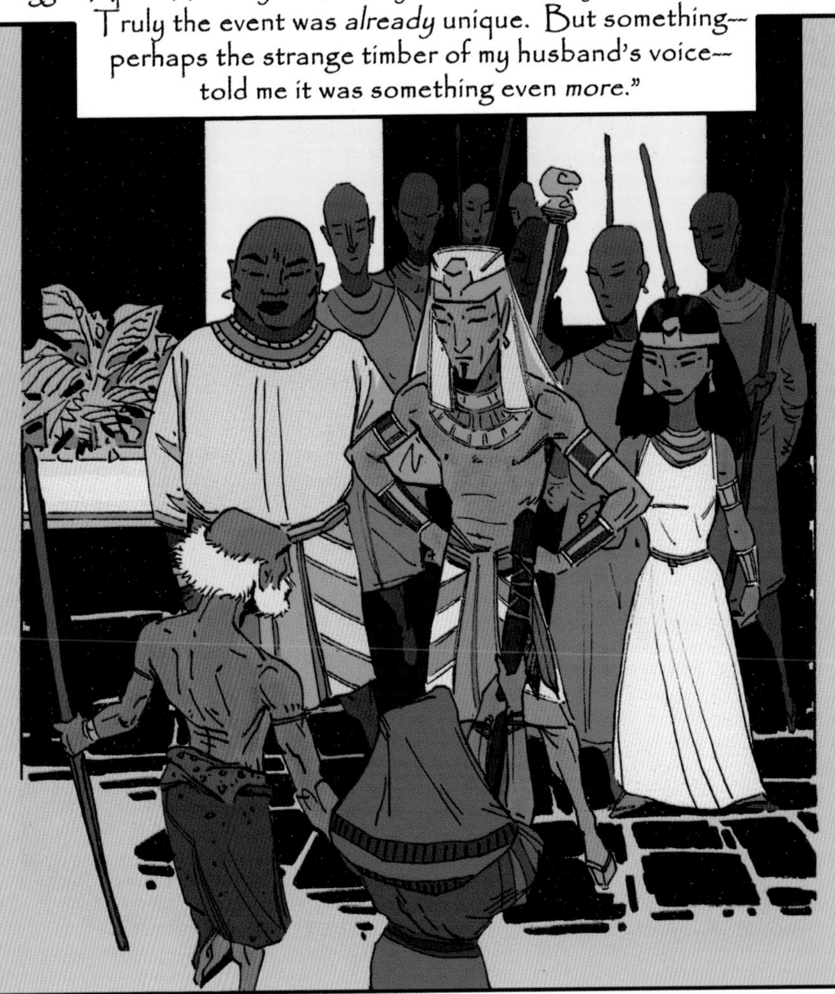
"The scene was strange, without question. The Pharaoh, the High Priest, and all the head clerics somberly assembling to hold court with a pair of ragged Apiru. Not only that, but my kinsmen actually seemed... *disturbed*. Truly the event was *already* unique. But something-- perhaps the strange timber of my husband's voice-- told me it was something even *more*."
"This pair of Apiru announced themselves as the sons of Amram and Jochebed. Actually, only one of them said this, declaring himself a priest of the Levite tribe named Aaron. The other did *not* identify himself... but he seemed known to my husband and Bekenkhonsu."
"Thus I was reintroduced to Moses— Ramses' lost cousin."

"The events which followed... They were a blur."
"Words were exchanged, demands made..."
"...And Wonders Performed."

"I did not know whether to trust my eyes."

"I had seen her before-- she looked like waves of air over fire. Like a graceful willow watching a flame approach. She told me only that the past was *forfeit*... and our future held *destruction*."

SHE HASN'T AWOKEN YET, GRANDFATHER?
...WILL SHE BE OKAY?

...SHE HAS STIRRED SOME...

THE PHYSICS SAY SHE PASSED OUT SIMPLY FROM EXHAUSTION.

I SAW THEM CARRY HER OUT OF YOUR MEETING WITH THOSE TWO MEN.

YES, YES, BUT ENOUGH OF THAT SUBJECT...

WHAT BRINGS YOU FROM YOUR ROOM BEFORE FIRST LIGHT, CHILD?

WELL...

...I WAS CONCERNED FOR GRANDMOTHER.

AND...

AND THE OTHER CHILDREN WERE SAYING WE WERE LEAVING *TOMORROW* FOR AVARIS...

THEY ARE CORRECT.

THEN... THEN WHEN WILL YOU AND I HAVE TIME TO GO *SWIM?*

"I dream."

"In my dream--"
"--I see... a boy-- No... I see... a man... a man ruling all of Egypt."
"He bears the name... Seti."
"This one... who rules along Niles's waters... He is not the first to bear this name..."
"...Might he be... the last..?"
"IS IT WISE FOR THE TWO OF YOU TO BE OUT HERE ALONE IN THE DARK, RAMSES?"

MOSES!
YOU... YOU COME FOR ME-- GONE FROM TRAITOR TO ASSASSIN NOW?
NOT COUNTING THAT SHADE WHICH WALKED THE PALACE TWO SCORE YEARS ERE, WHOSE EXISTENCE OF FALLACY I SLEW AND RECREATED.
"I see the children of Israel... they are lost in the desert."
WHAT? YOU SPEAK GIBBERISH.
NO, RAMSES, I SPEAK TRUTH. MY BROTHER AARON MAY DELIVER IT PLAINLY TO YOUR HOLLOW EARS.
I AM NEITHER, COUSIN.
THE MOSES YOU REMEMBER WAS A FICTION, PHARAOH. ONE FORGED BY YOUR AUNT WHEN SHE PULLED HIM FROM THE WATER... AND ADOPTED THE ISRAELITE BABY AS HER OWN.
"Lost for years. Years and years on end.. And their prophet... our lost kinsman."

"A-ADOPTED...?"

YES, RAMSES. YOU SEE THAT NOW, DON'T YOU? HOW IT WAS ALWAYS MY DESTINY TO BE WITH THEM... JUST AS IT IS YOURS TO STRUGGLE. PERHAPS-- BUT ULTIMATELY RELEASE THEM.
"MOSES, YOU ASKED THAT I GIVE LEAVE TO THE ISRAELITES TO GO AND WORSHIP 'YAHWEH' FOR THREE DAYS IN THE WILDERNESS."

"YET YOU GIVE ME NO REASON TO BELIEVE THAT THEY WOULD RETURN."

YAHWEH'S WILL AND WORD IS REASON ENOUGH, KING.
BEAR WITNESS, RAMSES-- BEGIN, BROTHER.

"...Moses... he dies without ever finding a home... without ever finding a grave."
"...And now... The sun comes."

YOUR MAGICKS DO NOTHING, LEVITE. MY CLERICS COUNTERED YOUR SNAKE-- AND AMON-RA HAS MORE THEN ENOUGH **MIGHT** TO FOIL WHATEVER COMES FROM YOUR WILD, **TRICKSTER** GOD.

"...the sun... rich and crimson..."

"...crimson... like blood... I see it..."

"...I see the future of Egypt."

Canto Two

"IF CIVILIZATION HAS BUT ONE NAME, AXOS, IT IS *AVARIS.*"

"THE SEAT OF POWER FOR THE PHARAOH'S DYNASTY. THE LUSH BEAUTY OF THE NILE'S DELTA."

"AND THE HUB TO THE MANY TRADE ROUTES YOU LEARN, MY APPRENTICE, FOR OUR SILKS."

YES, MASTER LISSOS, I SEE.
COME! COME AND SAVOR THE EFFICIENCY AND MARVELOUS TRANQUILITY OF ITS MARKETPLACE...

"THE PALACE STAFF IS AT YOUR COMMAND, PRINCE KHEPSESHEF."

YOU WILL CONTINUE TO CONDUCT YOURSELVES WITH DIGNITY, YET NOT CONFUSE ROYALTY WITH GLUTTONY.
MEALTIMES WILL GO ON AS BEFORE, BUT THE PALACE WILL UNDERGO THE SAME RATIONING AS THE CITIZENRY.
DURING THIS SHORTAGE, ALL FEASTS ARE CANCELLED.

--THE PHARAOH SENT OUT *MERCHANTS* TO ALL OUR NEIGHBORS FOR FRESH FISH AND WATER. BUT AS HIGH PRIEST I WILL *NOT* HAVE OUTSIDE MAGICIANS DO *YOUR* WORK AS THE CLERICS OF AMON-RA.
BUT BEKENKHONSU, OUR POWERS CAN BARELY REPLICATE THE ISRAELITE'S FEAT OF TURNING WATER TO BLOOD, MUCH LESS TURN IT *BACK*.

-- RETAIN ALL DIPLOMATIC RELATIONS, AND DO SO *WARILY*. EGYPT IS IN A TIME OF CRISIS, YES, BUT WE ARE *FAR* FROM WEAK OR DEFENSELESS. AS PHARAOH, I SAY THIS IS A TIME THAT WILL *PROVE* OUR STRENGTH AND DIVINE APPROVAL, RATHER THAN GIVE THIS *YAHWEH* AND MOSES--
MY LORD...?

...NEFERTARI--
HOW IS SHE?

SHE SWOONED AGAIN,
MY LORD AND HUSBAND.

ALL
YOUR WIVES
HAVE COME TO
TEND HER.
I--
...YES,GOOD. YOU
ARE ALL DUTIFUL AND MUCH
LOVED FOR YOUR--

...*Ramses*...?

NEFERTARI, MY LOVE... I AM HERE.
...i-it has happened again...?
"APPARENTLY SO, DEAR ONE."

SETI TOLD ME ONLY THAT YOU WERE SICK AGAIN.
IS THERE PAIN?
...has the Nile y-yet cleared...?

IT IS NOT AS IMPORTANT AS--
i-it is *crucial*, Ramses... m-much moreso than the h-health of one woman--

"e-even the queen."
...I...I WILL RETURN SOON, BELOVED...
"...REGAIN YOUR STRENGTH. THE KINGDOM NEEDS YOU."

...hmmm...I was going to s-say the same... to *you*...

I HAD THE ROOM CLEARED FOR YOU.

TA... YOU HAVE KNOWN **NEFERTARI** AS LONG AS I...
...IS ...IS THIS HER FATE?

"HAVE FAITH, RAMSES... I WILL LEAVE YOU TO YOUR THOUGHTS."

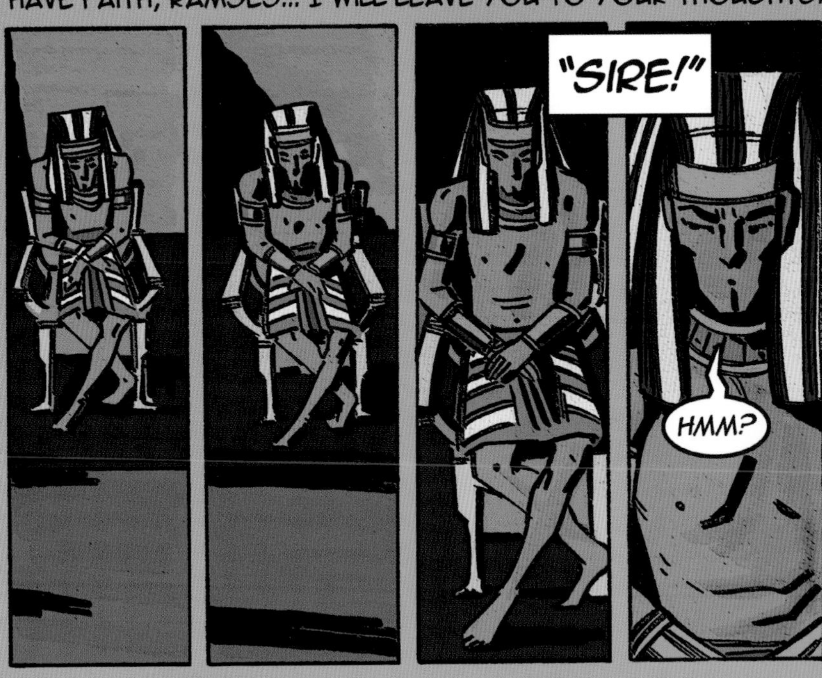

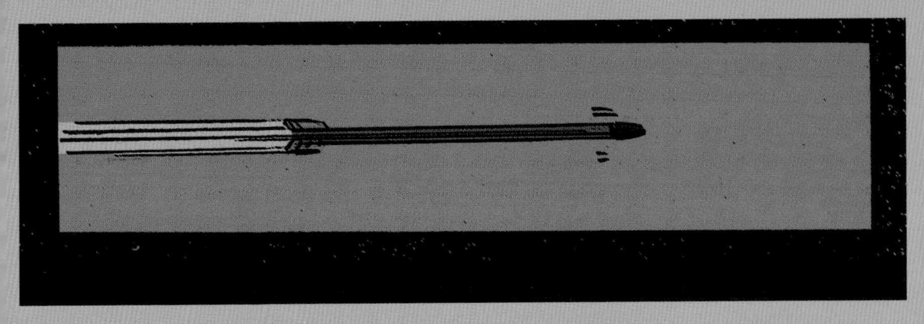

SCHHHWOKK!!!

"OUR CURSES HAVE COME ASHORE."

EVERY STREET AND PATH-- BLOCKED!
BY FROGS, BY THEIR CORPSES, BY THEIR GORE, AND BY THEIR EXCREMENT...!
THE DEATH-COUNT CLIMBS.
THEY SLICED THROUGH MY CEILING LIKE SPEARS-- A FROG SHATTERED MY TABLE LIKE A HAMMER.
ONLY GOSHEN IS UNTOUCHED.
ALL THE FROGS...
AN APIRU WIZARD CLAIMS HE SUMMONED THEM.
AMON-RA'S TEMPLES..
AVARIS...
MY BED...
BUT NOT GOSHEN?
ALL EGYPT, MAYBE...

ENOUGH!
TA.
NERFERTARI'S CHAMBERS...
ARE THEY CLEAR, AT LEAST?
JUST AS YOU ORDERED.

AS IS THE ISRAELITE ENCAMPMENT OF GOSHEN.
IT'S... UNNATURAL!
I CAN SUMMON A FROG, BUT I CAN'T DO THIS!
NONE OF THIS IS NATURAL, KHEPSESHEF.

REGARDLESS... DELIVERANCE BY AMPHIBIAN?
CAN THIS BE HIS PLAN?
SIRE?
JUST-- GAH... WE MUST SUMMON MOSES!

HE IS ALREADY HERE, RAMSES.
WHAT?

...CAUGHT A GLIMPSE OF THE TWO OF THEM IN THERE... FILTHY *APIRU!*
THAT SO? HMMMP.
A BIT MUCH HAVING BOTH OF US HERE.
IT COULD BE A DESERT RAT IN THERE, FOR ALL I CARE.
HEH, HEH! AS LONG AS WE'RE OFF FROG DETAIL...
I HEARD THAT SOME *APIRU* WIZARD CAUSED IT.
THE RIVER?
THE FROGS?
"...THINK OF THE POWER HE WOULD HAVE TO HAVE."

..THANK YOU, REBCHA...
MOSES...
DID I MISREPRESENT YOU IN THERE?
YOU SERVED THE SACRED WORDS OF *YAHWEH* FAITHFULLY, BROTHER.
THEN I ADMIT I AM AT A LOSS FOR WHAT JUST TRANSPIRED.
WE SAID WE WOULD LIFT THE PLAGUE *NOW* IN EXCHANGE FOR PHARAOH'S WORD *TOMORROW.*
BUT PHARAOH WILL *NOT* KEEP HIS WORD.
INDEED THE *LORD* HAS FURTHER WONDERS TO DEAL AGAINST EGYPT.
BESIDES...
WHEN IS A FROG, *NOT* A FROG?

THOSE JACKALS!
THE ISRAELITES...?
I WAS THERE TO ADVISE YOU! TO GUARD AGAINST THIS SORT OF... OF--
TA. MY WIFE IS SLEEPING. I WAS MEDITATING.
OUTSIDE.
AARON IS A LEVITE AND MOSES IS TRAINED AS MY ROYAL KINSMAN. THEIR WAYS WITH WORDS ARE PRODIGIOUS. TRICKERY WAS TO BE EXPECTED.
NNM.

"THEY REMOVED **ONLY** THE LIVING FROGS, AND LEFT THE CADAVERS."

HAH! SILVER-TONGUED DOGS!

YOU GIVE THEM TOO MUCH CREDIT.
WE'LL FIND A WAY TO HANDLE IT.

"you give them too much credit!"

TA?
you showed your hand when you spoke of them as "subjects".

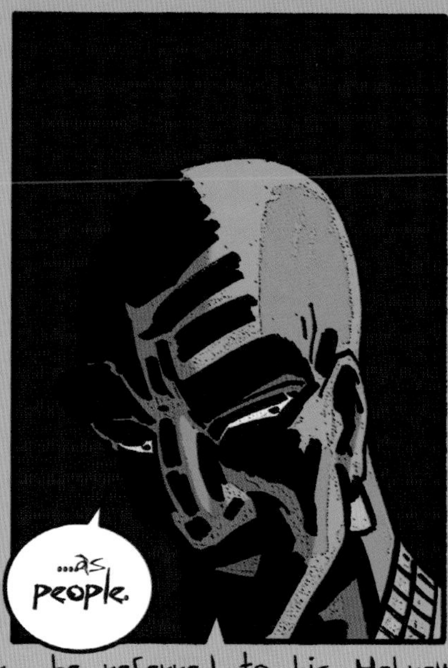
...as people.

I am reminded of your father... he referred to his Hebrew concubines as items. "Bring it to me, it pleased me." his father tamed the Israelites before their masses overwhelmed us. you've shown the Hittites our cancer.

FATHER, THE TASKMASTERS ARE READY TO RELEASE THE--

You will NOT release the Israelites, Ramses. You cannot. They will defy you as they defy Amon-Ra-- To release them is to raise an army against Egypt.

You must breach your pledge to Moses.

...FATHER?

"YOU HEARD MY CHIEF VIZIER," SON... HOLD THE ISRAELITES."

"MOSES?"

"HMMM?"

"THEY DID NOT ARRIVE... THEY ARE NOT COMING."

"YES, AARON, THEY ARE COMING."

"...MOSES, PHARAOH HAS GONE BACK ON HIS WORD, AS *YAHWEH* SAID. OUR TRIBESMEN ARE NOT YET BEING RELEASED."

"OH NO, ***NOT*** OUR TRIBESMEN..."

"THEN *WHO*...?"

"NOT WHO, AARON. *WHAT*."

"NOW AARON... STRETCH OUT YOUR STAFF."

"THE AIR FILLED WITH THEIR SICK HUM, INVADING EVERY HOME AND OPEN DOORWAY WITH THEIR STINGING BUZZ."

"THEY DESCENDED ON AVARIS LIKE A LIVING SANDSTORM."
"BUT PERHAPS IN THAT SOLE REGARD WE WERE LUCKY. AVARIS HAS PROCEDURES FOR WEATHERING A SANDSTORM-- "
"THE CITIZENRY KNEW HOW TO REACT, WHERE TO GO, WHAT TO DO."
"THUS ALL THE CITY-- AND PERHAPS THE NATION-- SHUT THEMSELVES IN...AND, IN THE OPPRESSIVE, HUMID DARKNESS, THEY WAITED."

"WAS THIS ALL A MATTER OF PATIENCE?"
"WERE WE CONSIGNED TO THESE ISRAELITE CURSES AND JUST NEEDED TO SEE THEM THROUGH?"
"THIS IS WHEN BEKENKHONSU CAME TO ME..."
MY LORD, I THINK IT WOULD BE WISEST FOR THE CLERICS AND I TO GO AND STAND GUARD BY NEFERTARI.

GIVE HIM TO ME, FATHER. COME TO ME, SETI.
FATHER!
SIRE.
GUARD THE QUEEN? YOU SUSPECT SHE IS IN PERIL?
HER AILMENT MAY BE MYSTICAL, SIRE. WE CAN PREVENT ANY FURTHER SORCERY BEFALL HER.
SEND HALF YOUR CLERICS TO HER SIDE, THEN. BUT THE REMAINDER MUST COMBAT--
SIRE... WE HAVE NOTHING TO COMBAT WITH!
...ALL THIS... IT GOES BEYOND EVEN OUR MINIMAL UNDERSTANDING!
THE POWER OF THIS YAHWEH...
AMON-RA HAS ABANDONED US, RAMSES.
FORSAKEN EGYPT
THIS IS BUT A FINGER OF THE ONE, TRUE GOD!

I RECALL HAVING A MONSTROUS HEADACHE FROM SHAME OF MOSES' OUTWITTING... BUT THE ***LAST*** THING WE WANT ARE THESE ***PLAGUED*** ISRAELITES IN OUR LAND ANY LONGER.

...ER... YES... QUITE RIGHT, TA.

"KHEPSESHEF WAS AS PUZZLED AS I. TA WAS SINCERE, NO DOUBT... AND SOMETHING ELSE ABOUT THIS MYSTERY FELT FAMILIAR."

I NEED...
I NEED TIME, GENTLEMEN.
"AND, WHILE TRAPPED INDOORS BY THE GNATS' ONSLAUGHT, WE HAD AN UNFORTUNATE SURPLUS OF THAT--"

--HOURS HAVE PASSED AND I STILL REMAIN AT A LOSS...
TA'S BEHAVIOR.
MOSES' SCHEMES.
HIS MOTIVES.
BEKENKHONSU'S...

"...I DO NOT KNOW WHAT TO DO, FATHER."

FATHER, FORGIVE THE INTRUSION...
...BUT THERE IS NEWS.
THIS MESSENGER HAS BRAVED THE... INSECTS TO DELIVER HIS REPORT.
..HRRK... TH-THE, NRG, SHORELINE... S-SIRE...
SLOWLY, GOOD MAN. SPEAK YOUR PIECE.
...TH-THEY ARE... KGH... D-DISPERSING BY THE SHORE...ONLY THE SH-SHORE...

YOU TAKE THIS TO BE A SIGN, FATHER?
MMM.
HE IS TAUNTING ME. HE KNOWS AMON-RA IS SILENT. HE WISHES ME TO COME ALONE.
I UNDERSTAND... YOU ARE AFRAID.
AFRAID?? THIS IS WHY WE NAMED YOU "STRONG ARM" AND NOT "STRONG MIND" BOY...!

I AM NOT MADE OF STONE, CERTAINLY, BUT I SHALL FACE HIM.

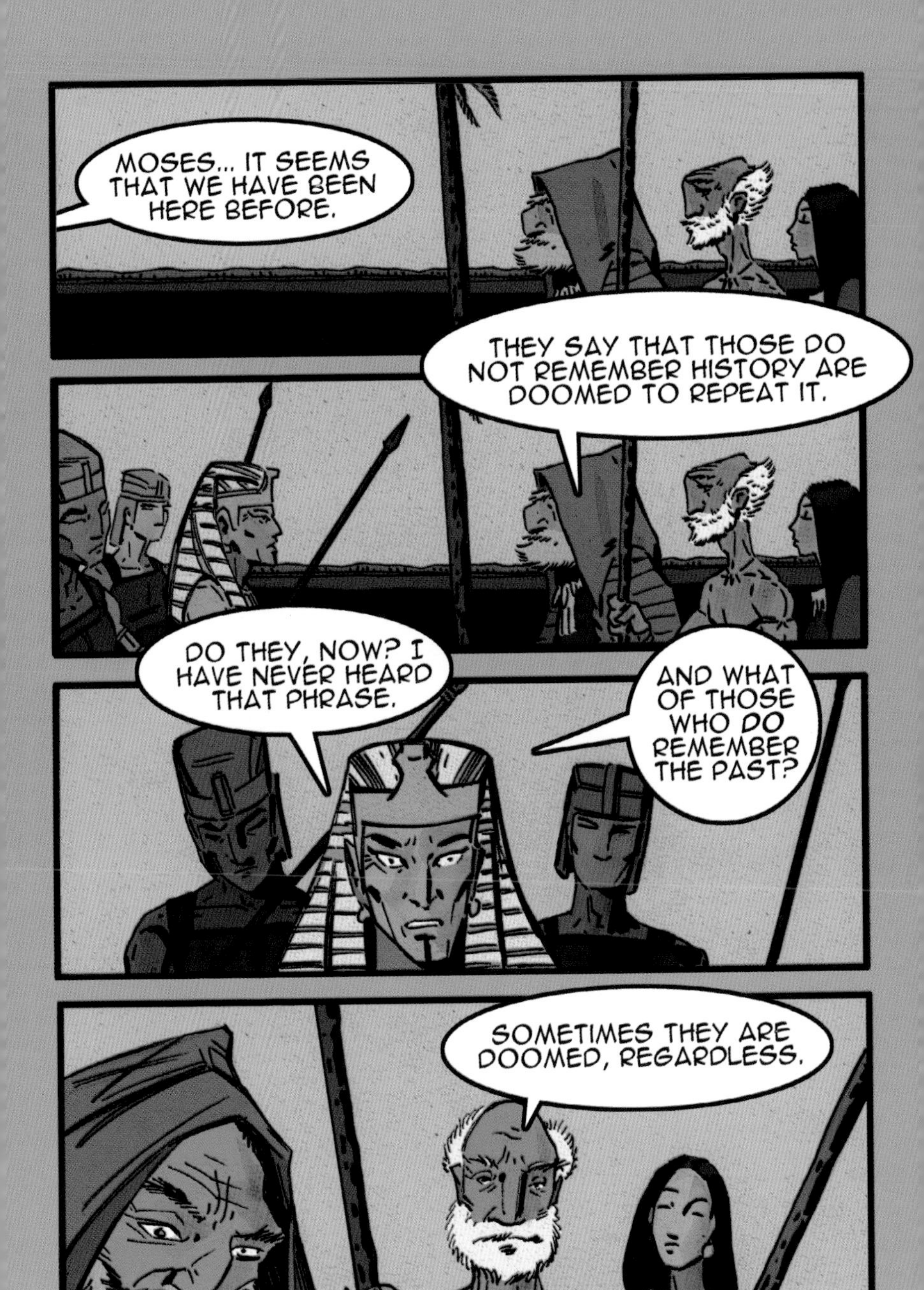
MOSES... IT SEEMS THAT WE HAVE BEEN HERE BEFORE.
THEY SAY THAT THOSE DO NOT REMEMBER HISTORY ARE DOOMED TO REPEAT IT.
DO THEY, NOW? I HAVE NEVER HEARD THAT PHRASE.
AND WHAT OF THOSE WHO *DO* REMEMBER THE PAST?
SOMETIMES THEY ARE DOOMED, REGARDLESS.

AND WHY HAVE YOU BROUGHT ME THIS CHILD?
"O MIGHTY PHARAOH," MEET THE FACE OF THE HEBREWS.
--REBCHA, MEET YOUR PHARAOH AND CAPTOR, RAMSES.
IT IS AN HON-- ...UM, A PLEAS-- ...MY L-LO-- ...SIRE. ER...SIR.
DO NOT SUBJECT ME TO FOOLISHNESS. MOSES. YOUR SORCERIES HAVE CUT A SWATH THROUGH THE GNATS FOR US TO ARRIVE HERE UNASSAILED.
WHAT DO YOU WANT?
SORCERERS WILL NEVER PROSPER-- BUT I AM AN EMISSARY FOR HE WHO IS CALLED "I AM" WHO DOES NOT WANT, BUT SIMPLY DELIVERS AND DOES.

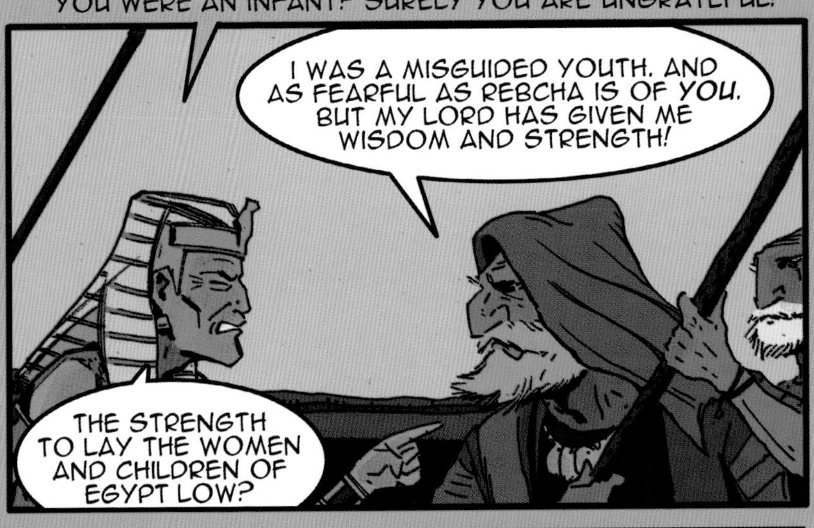
WHAT DO YOU BABBLE ON ABOUT?? HOW-- HOW CAN YOU DO THIS? DID MY OWN FAMILY BRING YOU UP WHEN YOU WERE AN INFANT? SURELY YOU ARE UNGRATEFUL!
I WAS A MISGUIDED YOUTH. AND AS FEARFUL AS REBCHA IS OF YOU. BUT MY LORD HAS GIVEN ME WISDOM AND STRENGTH!
THE STRENGTH TO LAY THE WOMEN AND CHILDREN OF EGYPT LOW?

NO LOWER THAN YOU HAVE THE ISRAELITES!
AND INFIRM YOUR OWN NIECE?
TO CAST SICKNESS OVER HER AS WELL?
NEFERTARI?
...I ...DID NOT KNOW SHE WAS ILL.
IT IS... IT IS NOT OF OUR DOING.

...WE COME TO BRING THE WORDS OF YAHWEH, WHO TELLS EGYPT TO LET HIS PEOPLE GO SO THAT WE MAY WORSHIP HIM.

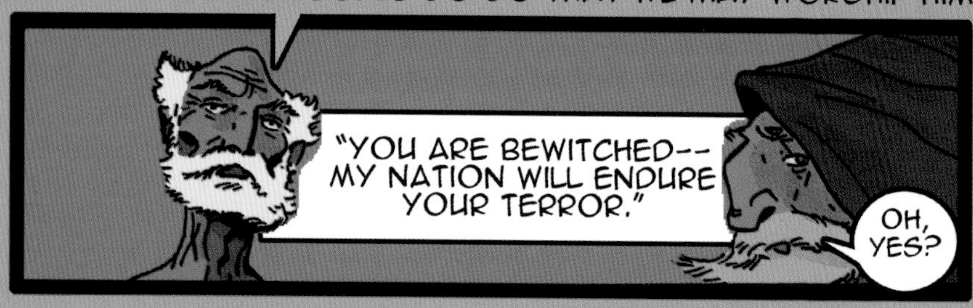

"YOU ARE BEWITCHED-- MY NATION WILL ENDURE YOUR TERROR."
OH, YES?

"YOU DO NOT ACKNOWLEDGE-- YOU DO NOT YET FEAR-- THE AUTHORITY OF THE ONE TRUE GOD. YOU STILL HOLD TO AN OUTDATED, OUTMODED, AND ILLUSORY FAITH. BUT YOU DO NOT EVEN LOOK TO YOUR AMON-RA TO SAVE YOU FROM YAHWEH... WHAT IS IT YOU FEAR, RAMSES?"

"PERHAPS...LOCUSTS?"
"YES, HUNGRY LOCUSTS... SWARMING SPEEDILY TOWARD YOUR LAND. TOWARD YOUR CROPS... YOUR FEEBLE, DWINDLING CROPS. THEY COME FOR YOUR FOOD."

"DIMINISHING WATER, SCARCE FOOD, VIRTUAL IMPRISONMENT WITHIN THEIR HOMES-- ...WHERE IS YOUR ***NATION*** NOW, PHARAOH?"

Canto Three

"IS THIS WHAT IS WRITTEN?"

"AM I... AM I DESTINED TO LOSE YOU, MY QUEEN?"

"MY OTHER WIVES-- THEY HONOR YOU."
"THEY KNOW YOU TO BE QUEEN, NONE WISHING TO SUPPLANT YOU."

"HAVE I STEERED US WISELY? COULD ONLY CATASTROPHE FOR EGYPT BE WHAT IS WRITTEN?"

"AND IF SO--"

"--WHAT CRUEL AUTHOR ASSIGNS US THIS FATE?"

"MOSES, HIS BROTHER, THEIR WHOLE BROOD... I WANTED TO BE RID OF THEM. BEKENKHONSU ADVISED AGAINST IT. KHEPSESHEF, TOO."

"BUT I SAW."
"EGYPT NEEDED TO BE FREE OF THE BLOOD CHOKING ITS NILE..."

"...AND OF THE FLIES AND GNATS INFESTING ITS AIR. ON CONDITION THAT THESE SORCERIES WOULD ABATE, WOULD BE *REMOVED*--"

"--I GRANTED MOSES AND HIS SWARM THEIR THREE DAYS OUTSIDE THE CITY LIMITS."
"TROOPS COULD RECLAIM THEM IF NEED BE, EVEN BLOCKADE THEIR RETURN AND LET THEM COOK UNDER AMON-RA'S EYE A FEW DAYS MORE."

"IT WAS NOT UNTIL THAT EVENING, DURING MY MEDITATIONS THAT I FOUND OUT HOW TRULY INFECTIOUS THE HEBREW BLIGHT WOULD BE."
...WHO--?

grandfather.
SETI, CHILD? IS THAT YOU...?

"...HOW TRULY DIABOLICAL..."

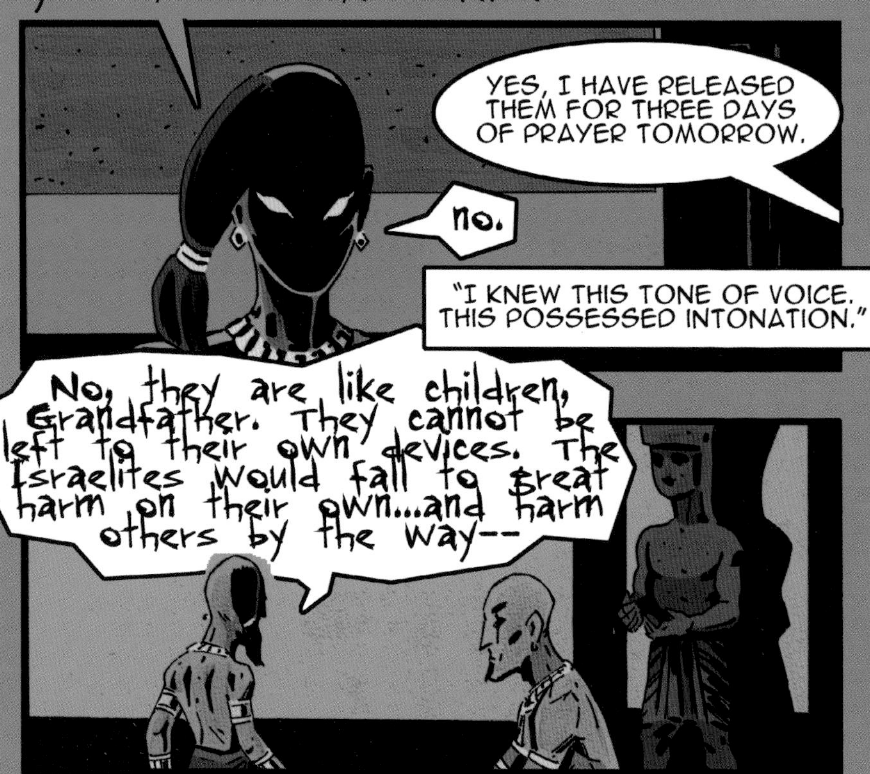

you think on the israelites.
YES, I HAVE RELEASED THEM FOR THREE DAYS OF PRAYER TOMORROW.
no.
"I KNEW THIS TONE OF VOICE. THIS POSSESSED INTONATION."
No, they are like children, Grandfather. They cannot be left to their own devices. The Israelites would fall to great harm on their own...and harm others by the way--

"THIS VOICE CAME TWICE BEFORE. ONCE FROM A GUARDSMAN, AND AGAIN FROM MY VIZIER."
--Harm those whom you care for, grandfather.

"AND NOW SOME SPLINTER OF THE HEBREW DEMON HAD INFECTED OUR FAMILY AND HELD SETI IN ITS POWER. THE MESSAGE OF YAHWEH WAS CLEAR."

"AMON-RA WAS POWERLESS TO DEFEND US, MY HEART. I HAD BUT ONLY ONE RECOURSE."

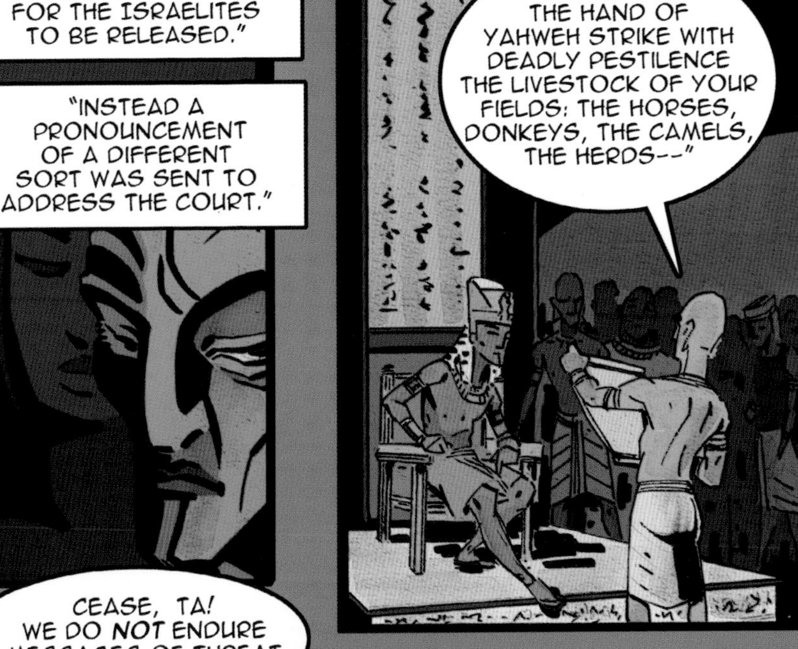

"THE NEXT DAY, I GAVE NO ORDER FOR THE ISRAELITES TO BE RELEASED."
"INSTEAD A PRONOUNCEMENT OF A DIFFERENT SORT WAS SENT TO ADDRESS THE COURT."
"...THUS WILL THE HAND OF YAHWEH STRIKE WITH DEADLY PESTILENCE THE LIVESTOCK OF YOUR FIELDS: THE HORSES, DONKEYS, THE CAMELS, THE HERDS--"

CEASE, TA! WE DO NOT ENDURE MESSAGES OF THREAT FROM ISRAELITES.
THEY DO NOT HOLD THE WHIP!
WE HAVE WITNESSED THEIR DARK MAGICKS, PRINCE KHEPSESHEF.
WE WILL BE READY.

"SILENTLY, I LISTENED, ALLOWING MY SON HIS MOMENT AS REGENT--AS MY FATHER DID WITH ME. THE STRONG PRINCE GAVE HIS PLAN..."

"OUR SON KNEW THE ISRAELITE WARNING TO BE NO BLUFF. NEITHER DID HE PRESUME IT TO BE ABSOLUTE. THEY COULD NOT SLAY WHAT THEY COULD NOT ACCESS-- AND SO, FENCES WERE BUILT AROUND A PORTION OF THE CATTLE."
"THEY COULD NOT SLAY WHAT THEY COULD NOT FIND, PRESUMED KHEPSESHEF-- AND SO, HERDS WERE LED OUT TO THE BORDERS OF OUR LAND AND DEEP INTO THE CELLARS OF THE CITIZENS' LARGER DOMICILES."
"THE ISRAELITES COULD NOT SLAY WHAT WE HAD ALREADY BUTCHERED-- AND SO, THE LAST OF OUR LIVESTOCK WAS HURRIEDLY SLAUGHTERED FOR STORAGE AND COOKING."
"SO TELLING OF OUR SON'S STRENGTH TO ONE DAY LEAD EGYPT! IT WAS A GOOD PLAN. IT WAS A DECISIVE PLAN--"

"AND IT WAS ALL FOR NAUGHT."
"AS IF ON AN INVISIBLE CUE, ALL OF THE BARRICADED SHEEP AND CATTLE LAY DOWN TO SLEEP... NEVER TO RISE AGAIN."
"FROM THE CELLARS IN THE HEART OF OUR LANDS AND THE PADDOCKS ON OUR BORDERS FAMILIES CRIED AS ONE TO FIND THEIR FLOCKS EMBRACED BY ANUBIS."
"THOSE WHO DID NOT SEE IT, SOON EXPERIENCED ITS STENCH-- AS THE VERY FOOD ON THEIR TABLES SPOILED AS QUICKLY AS A DOUSED FIRE."

"ALL OF OUR LIVESTOCK, NO MATTER WHERE IT LAY, PERISHED... WHILE THE ISRAELITES' MEAGER CATTLE SURVIVED. THEIR GOD, THEIR YAHWEH, WAS TRULY WITH THEM. OUR PEOPLE NOW FEARED THEM, HATED THEM, EVEN FURTHER."

"THE ISRAELITES HAD A POWER THAT WE HAD TO KEEP IN CHECK, A POWER OUR PRIESTS COULD NOT COUNTER."

"OUR CLERGY, SENT TO SPEAK WITH MOSES, FELL FIRST WHEN THE BOILS CAME."

"THEN THE SORES CAME TO THE WHOLE OF THE PEOPLE, AND THERE WAS NOTHING WE COULD DO..."

"...BUT SLEEP."

PHARAOH!
RAMSES!
NNN...
T-TA?
...I THOUGHT--
I AM SORRY TO WAKE YOU, BUT...

...THEY HAVE RETURNED, SIRE.

"MOSES AND AARON AWAITED ME IN THE THRONE ROOM."

"BUT THERE WAS A DIFFERENCE IN THEIR RETURN. PERHAPS IN ME, OR PERHAPS IN THEM."
"THE SCALES OF SHAI HAD CERTAINLY SHIFTED."

YOUR BOILS LOOK PAINFUL. DO THEY MAKE SPEAKING DIFFICULT?
I ENDURE, HEBREW.

NOW HAS YOUR BROTHER COME TO SPEAK WITH ME--

--OR HAVE YOU COME ONLY TO REJOICE IN THE SUFFERING OF THE EGYPTIAN MEN AND WOMEN?

"I ALLOWED THEM TO DEPART. HOLDING THEM WOULD ONLY CAUSE GREATER CALAMITY. AND FRANKLY, NEFERTARI, FOR THE FIRST TIME, I FEARED WHAT GREATER CATASTROPHE WOULD ENSUE."

SIRE... OUR PRIESTS-- I HAVE OVERHEARD THEM, PHARAOH, SPEAKING...SPEAKING HERESIES. CALLING YAHWEH, THE LORD OF AARON AND MOSES THE LORD OF THE UNIVERSE.

I WOULD LIKE TO SUGGEST THE FOLLOWING COURSE OF ACTION, PRINCE KHEPSESHEF.
BEKENKHONSU!
SPEAK TO ME AGAIN OF YOUR FAITHLESS PRIESTS AND I WILL CUT OFF YOUR HANDS, YOUR FEET AND IMPALE YOU IN THE TEMPLE OF AMON-RA!

"I UNLEASHED AN UNFAIR WRATH ON BEKENKHONSU, BUT I COULD HOLD IT NO MORE. I WANTED TO TERRORIZE HIM, I REALIZE-- I WANTED RESPECT AGAIN, EVEN IF I COULD ONLY ELICIT IT FROM HIS FEAR."

"NOT RESPECT. **CONTROL.** I NEEDED CONTROL RESTORED."

...FACE ME, TYRANT... STOP HIDING BEHIND YOUR EMISSARIES... YOUR PLAGUES.
FACE ME!
FATHER! SIRE, GET INSIDE!

YOU CAN'T BE OUT THERE. YOU ARE NOT INDESTRUCTABLE.
I HAVE ALREADY BEEN LED TO THAT CONCLUSION, SON.
I ONLY MEANT THAT THE HAIL WAS PUMMELING THE ENTIRETY OF OUR LAND.

"~*THE ENTIRETY OF OUR LAND...*
EXCEPT GOSHEN, THE ISRAELITE PORTION OF THE CITY. THEIR NEST. IT WAS THE ONLY PLACE WHERE THE HAIL DID NOT FALL."

IT'S-- IT'S...THE ELDERS MUST ALLY WITH THE SONS OF AMRAM NOW, REBCHA

"OUR CURSE WAS THEIR MIRACLE."

"THE PRESENCE THAT HAD HELD OUR GRANDSON RELEASED ITS GRIP AT LAST."

"BUT WITH THE BOILS STILL UPON US I KNEW OUR TRIALS WERE NOT OVER."

WE ARE DELIVERED! THE HAIL HAS ABATED. AND THOUGH THE BARLEY AND FLAX CROPS HAVE BEEN RUINED, THE LATE-BLOOMING SPELT CROPS HAVE ENDURED!

SOME RELIEF AT LEAST, THANK THE GODS.
Y-YES, SIRE. WE HAVE BEEN SPARED.

INDEED. PRAISE AMON-RA, YES, BEKENKHONSU?
W-WE...I, ER... A P-PRESENCE CERTAINLY, UH, EMBRACES EGYPT, SI--
"YAHWEH"

"BEKENKHONSU, HIS FAITH SHATTERED, MEANT YAHWEH. HE WAS LOST."
SAY NO MORE, BEKENKHONSU. I WILL SHOW THE ISRAELITES THE TRUE FACE OF THIS PHARAOH--

"--HAVE THEM SUMMONED," I SAID. I ASK FOR YOUR STRENGTH, MY QUEEN. I FEAR FOR MY PRIDE. I QUESTION MY WISDOM--
--IN INVITING THEM HERE.
...THE PHARAOH'S OWN BED CHAMBERS!....

WE WILL AWAIT OUR PEOPLE TO BE RELEASED PAST GOSHEN.

"...FAREWELL, RAMSES."

...RAMSES.
MY NIECE, NEFERTARI. HOW DOES SHE FARE?
NO BETTER THAN MOST, MOSES
SHE IS DYING.
PHARAOH. I HOPE YOU KNOW, PHARAOH, THAT--
...I AM SORRY, PHARAOH.
...
PRIEST... MY NAME IS RAMSES.

FINALLY, HE SLEEPS.
OUR HUSBAND SHOWS SUCH DEDICATION TO HIS QUEEN.

--HOW CAN YOU NOT ADMIRE HIS--
NEFERTARI!
MMM...NHH
...NNN...? BINT-ANATH, MY WIFE, WHAT...?
RAMSES! OUR QUEEN STIRS

NEFERTARI. MY LOVE, CAN--CAN YOU HEAR ME?

LET ME CALL A PHYSIC, BELOVED, TO AID YOUR--
shh...no, n-no, my king.
j-just be with me...

just be with me... u-until i go...
NO!
Y-YOU ARE--
YOU WILL RECOVER, MY QUEEN.

my dear heart, the kingdom will h-have her queen again...
...but it will not be me....

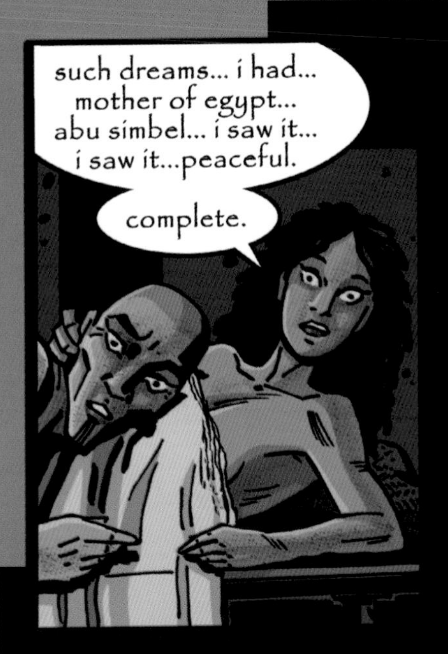
such dreams... i had...
mother of egypt...
abu simbel... i saw it...
i saw it...peaceful.
complete.

is it raining?
NO, MY QUEEN. NOT RAIN--
--IT IS HAIL...?

NEFERTARI, THE BOILS, THE HAIL-- GONE!
MOSES HAS FULFILLED HIS PLEDGE. AND NOW WE CAN BE FREE OF THE ISRAELITE PLAGUES.

no, ramses...
the israelites cannot be set free.

You dwell on your legacy, Lord of Shai and creator of Renenet. And rightly so.
MY QUEEN... YOUR VOICE IT'S...
NO, NO...
History will remember you, Pharaoh, King of Kings.
You must remain hard, Ozymandias.

Hear the words of your queen,
Ramses: the slaves must still remain

...A-AS MY QUEEN WISHES.
"THE ISRAELITES WILL BE HELD."

MEN AND WOMEN OF GOSHEN! I COME WITH MY BROTHER AND YOUR ELDERS-- I COME WITH THE WORDS OF YOUR LORD AND CREATOR!
IN THE YEARS OF FREEDOM THAT AWAIT US YOU MAY TELL YOUR CHILDREN AND YOU MAY TELL YOUR GRANDCHILDREN HOW *YAHWEH* MADE FOOLS OF THE EGYPTIANS.
YOU MAY TELL THEM OF THE WICKED PHARAOHS WHO BROKE THEIR WORD TO JOSEPH, WHO **ENSLAVED** OUR PEOPLE FOR TOO LONG, ONLY TO HAVE HIS **WRATH** BROUGHT UPON THEM, SIGN AFTER SIGN.
"THE EGYPTIANS ARE NOT OUR KIN. THEY ARE NOT THE INNOCENT. THEY ARE AND WILL HENCEFORTH ONLY BE... OUR *PAST!*"

EVEN IN HOLDING BACK OUR MEN FROM PRAYER THE EGYPTIANS HAVE UNITED US.

THEY HAVE BROUGHT OUR TRIBES TOGETHER UNDER THEIR OPPRESSION.

THEY HAVE ... LEFT US FREE FROM... FREE FROM...
UH...FROM CRUELTY! FREE FROM THEIR WHIPS, MY BROTHERS! FREE FROM--
INTRUDERS.

HOLD YOUR MEN, MOSES--

--WE YIELD.
THE PHARAOH!
SON OF AMON-RA.

IT *IS* THE PHARAOH!
THE SON OF SETI THE FIRST, BOTH OF THEM MORTAL MEN.
SAVE YOUR WORSHIP FOR ITS TRUE PLACE.

SO, RAMSES, AGAIN YOU BREAK YOUR OATH, THIS TIME TO INFILTRATE OUR RANKS?
YOU KNOW WELL THE REASON FOR MY RETRACTION--AND WHAT OF YOUR HOME-GROWN ARMY HERE, MOSES?
HAVE YOU GIVEN THEM THE GENERAL THEY DESIRE?
HAVE YOUR LACKEYS BACK OFF, COUSIN.
SON OF RAMSES, YOU BRING THE ONLY LACKEY HERE WITH YOU. AND FOR WHAT? TO BLUFF AND BLUSTER OUTSIDE THE SPACE OF YOUR PALACE?
NO, COUSIN. I HAVE COME TO SAY THIS:
MEN OF ISRAEL, GO... WORSHIP YAHWEH THE LORD!

ISRAELITE SLAVES!
I HARDEN MY HEART TO YOU!
YOU SHALL NOT LEAVE!

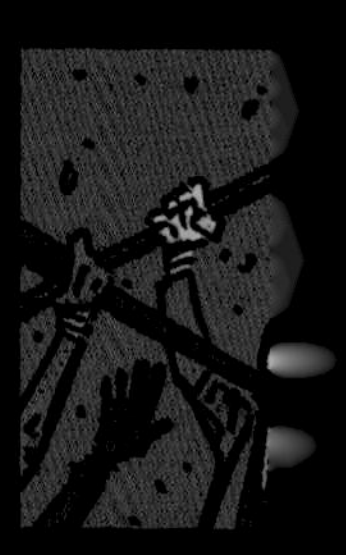

Canto Four

Two days later...
Only the Pharaoh and his Vizier Ta emerged from Goshen unscathed.
HAVE THEIR BODIES ADDED TO THE PROCESSION. IT... IS ONLY FITTING.
THEY DIED SO THAT PHARAOH AND I COULD SURVIVE THE APIRU MOB.
THEY WILL DEFEND HER KA FROM SET.
Worse news greeted their return.
AS YOUR BROTHER SPEAKS FOR YOU, MOSES, I SPEAK FOR PHARAOH.
YOUR LOCUSTS HAVE TAKEN THE LAST OF OUR CROPS. NOW TAKE YOUR PEOPLE FROM OUR LAND AS WELL.
WE HAVE SINNED. WE ASK FOR YAHWEH'S FORGIVNESS-- AND YOUR DEPARTURE.
The sons of Jochebed gave no acknowledgment.
They did not speak of the deaths.
They did not ask of the queen.

Ramses had not arisen to view the locusts. He had not given audience to the latest Hittite message.

SIRE. I HAVE SPOKEN WITH THE ISRAELITES. WITH MOSES.
...RAMSES?
...THE PATHS WRITTEN... ISRAEL LAID WASTE, YET HIS SEED IS NOT... DESTINY TO STRUGGLE...

He did not eat, did not sleep, did not move from his throne. His only words had been to himself.

...FALL TO GREAT HARM ON THEIR OWN... AND HARM OTHERS BY THE WAY...

The queen was dead...
and with her seemed to depart his soul.

Only one thing could shake him from his cloud of grief.

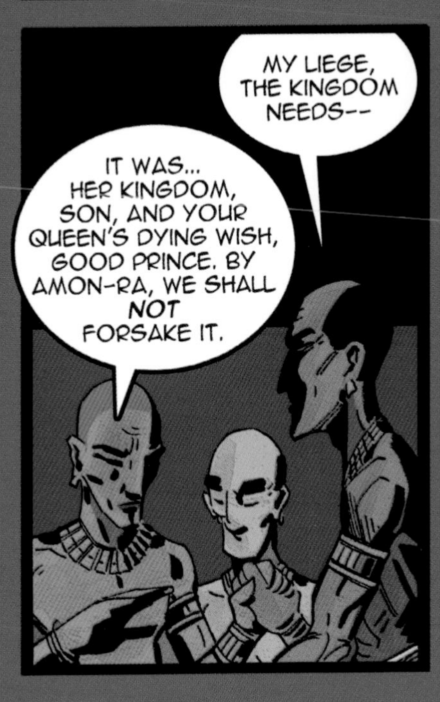

AND MAY THIS EYE SOON PASS FROM US.

The Pharaoh, his Vizier Ta, his wives and children, his High Priest Bekenkhonsu, Prince Khepseshef, young Prince Seti, counselors, soldiers, dignitaries, palace workers, the Great Powers of Egypt.
All in procession for distant Abu Simbel. All in the name of the late Queen Nefertari and her posthumous guards. All business and all activity in Avaris at a halt.

But at sunrise, all their mourning--

--was greeted by no morning.

...THE LIGHT DIES!

The screams were deafening.

The darkness absolute.

Oil would not burn.

Tinder would not catch.

Flame could not live.

The Egyptian nation was struck blind. Mothers groped from room to room for their crying children.

The last of the food had to be sniffed out.

The palace was a labyrinth.

RAMSES!

GRAND-FATHER?

SETI!

FATHER?

HERE, KHEPSESHEF. WE ARE HERE, SON.

HERE, MEN! PHARAOH IS--

I AM HERE, FATHER.

SETI!

I HAVE KEPT HIM WITH ME SINCE THIS BEGAN.

HOW LONG--?

NO WAY TO KNOW.

DAYS?

HAVE YOU EATEN?

WE HAD ENOUGH.

BEKENKHONSU SAID TO MAKE PREPARATIONS... TO EXPECT THE ISRAELITES.

DID HE SAY TO PRAY, FATHER?

NO, SETI.

TA?

HERE, RAMSES.

HE IS COMING.

MY LORD, RAMSES?

MY FRIEND, TA.

ASSESS OUR SUPPLIES. BE MINDFUL OF HEMLOCK.

OF COURSE, PHARAOH. WE WILL AVOID ITS PUNGENCY.

NO. HAVE IT BROUGHT HERE.

BUT...

IN THIS DARKNESS, ALL I KNOW IS THE TOUCH OF SETI'S HAND. WE ARE AS THOUGH NO LONGER REAL. I WOULD HAVE US CHOOSE OUR OWN ENDS...

RATHER THEN HAVE IT PRESCRIBED, AS IT WAS FOR NEFERTARI.

SIRE, LOOK!
LIGHT!
IT COMES FROM OUTSIDE.
LOOK!
...AND... CHANTING...

At the sight of the hideous, skull-topped pikes, they grew only angrier.

SSSK......BEKENKHONSU... ...THOSE SKULLS ARE HIS PREPARATIONS...?
TRULY? IT IS... BARBARIC...
SUMMONED NOT BY YOU, NOT BY YOUR SO-CALLED SON OF RA--
SUMMONED BY THAT BEING WHICH SPOKE UNTO MY HUMBLE FORM, BURNING IN THE BRUSH AS IT MUST STILL IN THE NIGHT OF THESE HORRIBLE SPECTERS...

SUMMONED BY ***YAHWEH***, THE ***NAME***, WHO RAGES AT YOUR DESECRATION OF THESE MEN.
AN ACT WHICH COULD NOT ESCAPE HER ALL SEEING GAZE EVEN UNDER THE CRUSHING BLANKETS OF NIGHT THAT VISIT THE EGYPTIAN PEOPLE.
MAKING HIS SCOURGE UPON YOUR HOUSE ALL THE MORE FITTING.
HMMP. "***HIS***", EH, MOSES.
<SIGH> IT MATTERS NOT, MIRIAM...

Even from high atop his balcony, Ramses could neither ignore Aaron nor his own still-fresh scratches and bruises.

WE ARE THE LIGHT OF THE WORLD, A FLAME THAT CANNOT BE SNUFFED.

YOU ARE A WILDFIRE, ISRAELITE, THAT WOULD CONSUME ALL IT ENCOUNTERS!
SON, NO... WE MUSTN'T--

From somewhere Ramses heard the rustle of a page, the intoning of a voice, the odd crackling of a rock.

From his own home and under siege, the Pharaoh braced himself for what must be done.

GO, SERVE THE LORD! YOUR CHILDREN MAY ALSO GO WITH YOU.

"PLAGUE US NO MORE, ISRAELITES."

BE PRAISED!
TRIUMPH IN THE NAME OF ISRAEL!
HONOR TO THE HOUSE OF AMRAM!
EGYPT IS MIGHTY, RAMSES. THEY ARE JUST WORDS, NOTHING MORE.

"NO, TA. THERE IS MORE."

Ramses could not see Moses from his position, but he knew his cousin's voice was not amongst the Israelite crowd.

He felt the aged man's gaze upon him and sensed Moses still turning strategy over and over again in his head.

The Pharaoh could not help but wonder: what was left to come.

CAN WE LOOK FOR IWIW, NOW?
IWIW...

The boy-prince's dog.

The animals.
ONLY, LET YOUR FLOCKS AND HERDS REMAIN BEHIND!
AHHH... SO WE CONTINUE...
THEY MUST LET US HAVE SACRIFICES AND BURNT OFFERINGS FOR THE LORD OUR GOD!
NOTHING MUST HAPPEN SAVE WHAT I DECREE, APIRU!
NOT A HOOF SHALL BE LEFT BEHIND!
NO! GET AWAY FROM ME...
...AND THE PALACE!
GIVE THE SIGNAL, AARON. WE RETURN TO GOSHEN EVEN AS THEIR LIGHT RETURNS TO THEM.
BUT--
WE HAVE HEARD ALL WE NEED TO, I ASSURE YOU.

And Ramses is certain of nothing.

YOUR PLOY IS MY FATHER'S LEGACY. JUST AS THE SLAVES ARE MY GRANDFATHER'S. PRAY HISTORY FORGETS YOU, OLD PRIEST.

HA-SHEM SMILES UPON US, REBCHA. THE EGYPTIANS TAKE NO NOTICE OF US.
OH, THEY NOTICE US, SETH.
AS SISTER MIRIAM SAID: THEY NOW FEAR REPRISAL.
AND WHILE SOME ARE JUST AND OTHERS MAY FEEL GUILT...
MANY ARE BEWILDERED BY THIS REVERSAL OF FORTUNE.
ISRAELITE! WAIT!
BUT WITH THE DIVINE'S WRATH UPON THEM, MOST SIMPLY FEAR US, AND WISH US GONE.
TAKE THIS BLANKET FOR YOUR JOURNEY!
UHHH...
AND THESE COINS. GOLD COINS!
...BEWILDERING.

The Egyptians could make no sense of the Israelites' preparations. They took no pains to hide their activities from their captors.
HE WASHES BLOOD ON HIS DOOR-WAY?

"AND INSIDE--THEY HURRY EVEN THE BREAD. THEIR BULLS, THEIR RAMS, ALL SORTED FROM THE REST OF THEIR FLOCKS."
BIZZARE APIRU...

... AND THE LEVITE, A-HARON... THEY DOUSE HIM IN OIL. THEY BURN ENTRAILS TO THEIR GOD.
AARON IS ALREADY MAKING SACRIFICES TO THEIR YAHWEH? I THOUGHT THAT WAS THE WHOLE POINT OF THEIR REBELLION...

HAS THIS ALWAYS BEEN ABOUT LIBERATING HIS NATION? IS THAT WHY ALL THE--
MMHH.
Ta knew that his friend was not listening.

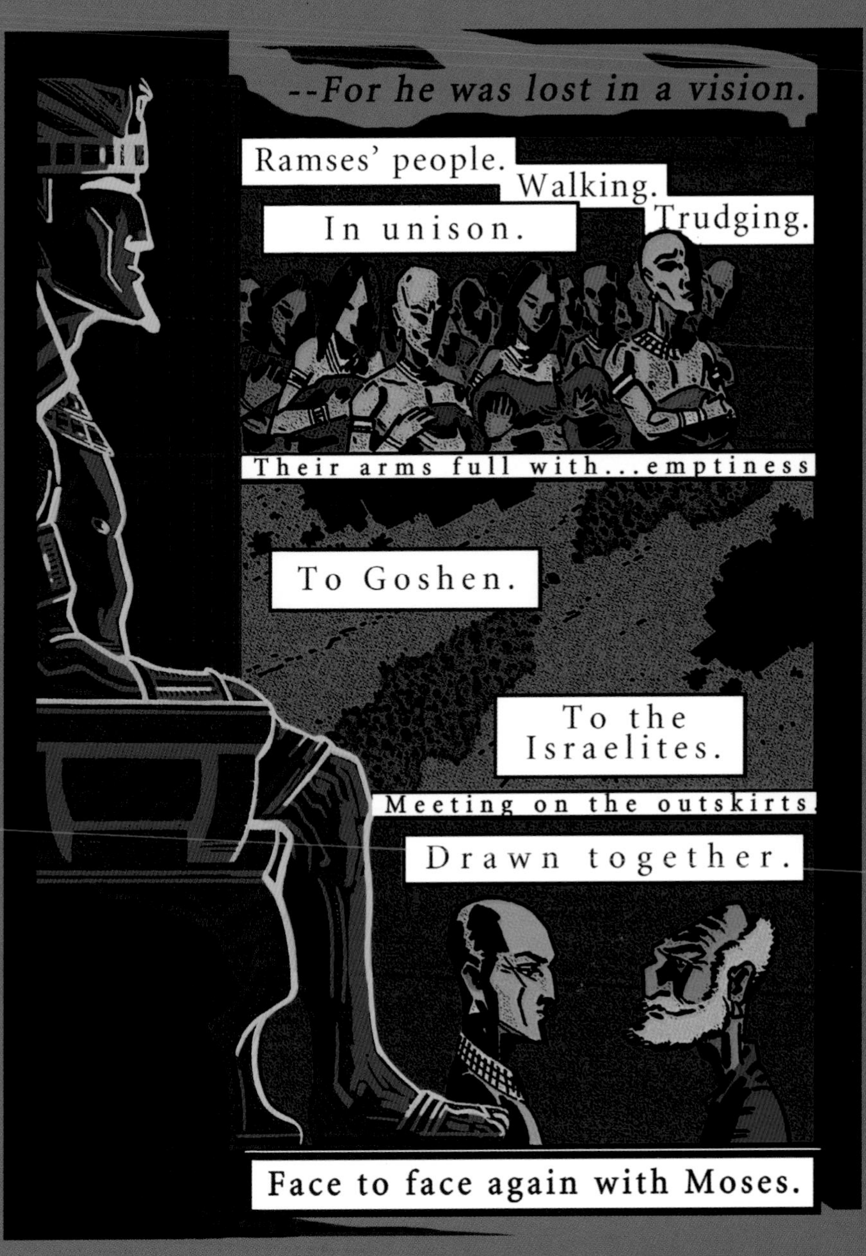

--For he was lost in a vision.
Ramses' people.
Walking.
Trudging.
In unison.
Their arms full with...emptiness
To Goshen.
To the Israelites.
Meeting on the outskirts.
Drawn together.
Face to face again with Moses.

Neither leader holding to his last threat.
Neither leader holding an advantage.
Nor a victory...

The vision passes,
leaving no explanation in its wake.
At the sound of his grandson's voice, his heir's kind tones, Ramses finally stirred and rejoined his remaining family.
Food was scarce, and evening was coming. But, for the first time in many days, there was joy.
Ramses' many wives, children and grandchildren knew that the crisis was over and the worst had been borne.
GRAND-FATHER...? WILL YOU JOIN US?
The humble meal was a feast in honor of their King, who had once again provided them with safety.
HE RARELY TIRES SO EASILY.
For a time, Ramses almost shared in their delight.

OH FATHER! CAST OFF THAT WORN EXPRESSION. YOU SAVED THE KINGDOM BY SACRIFICING YOUR PRIDE--

ME OR SETI, MY SON?

--AND IN DOING SO, YOU MADE YOUR FAMILY ITSELF PROUD.

HMM. I DOUBT YOUR GRANDFATHER WOULD AGREE, FRANKLY.

BUT "WE FOLLOW THE PATHS THAT ARE WRITTEN FOR US," I SUPPOSE.

IF NOTHING ELSE, MAY YOU AND YOUR SON LEARN FROM MY MISSTEPS. HOW TO LEAD OUR LAND TO BETTER DAYS WHEN YOU EACH ARE PHARAOH WHEN I HAVE PASSED.

MAY THAT DAY BE STILL FAR OFF, FATHER, AS I REMAIN YOUR "STRONG RIGHT ARM" AND YOU REMAIN MY KING.

HEH, YOU EVER REMAIN MY LITTLE APRICOT.

-- THOUGH AS MY FATHER ALSO SAID, "ALL FRUIT RIPENS".

TAKE YOUR SON TO BED, KHEPSESHEF, AND TOMORROW WE WILL DISCUSS YOUR CO-REGENCY.

I-- YES, SIRE. GOOD NIGHT, SIRE.

Tomorrow will be a new day for Egypt, thought Pharaoh. He saw nothing left to lose, nothing more to suffer. His mind could return to governing.

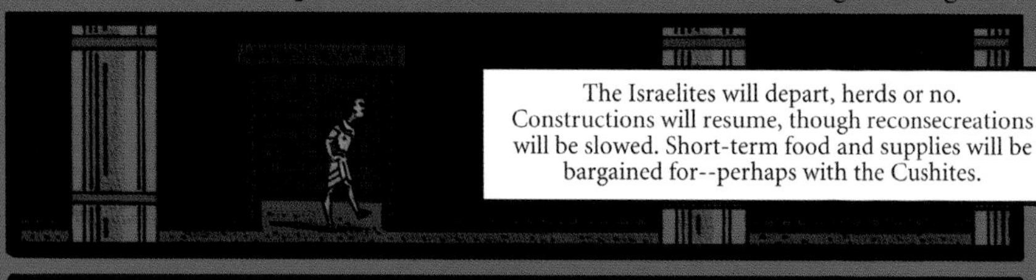

The Israelites will depart, herds or no. Constructions will resume, though reconsecreations will be slowed. Short-term food and supplies will be bargained for--perhaps with the Cushites.

Then there is the matter of the Hittites, but that can be negotiated. The treaty will hold, and they will look kindly on our losses...
Ramses thought on Nefertari and, for the first time, smiled. He knew her *ka* to be safe, and he thought of the joy Khepseshef's wisdom would have brought her.

Truly, Khepseshef's coming to power will be the greatest prize that Egypt--

FFWUMPP

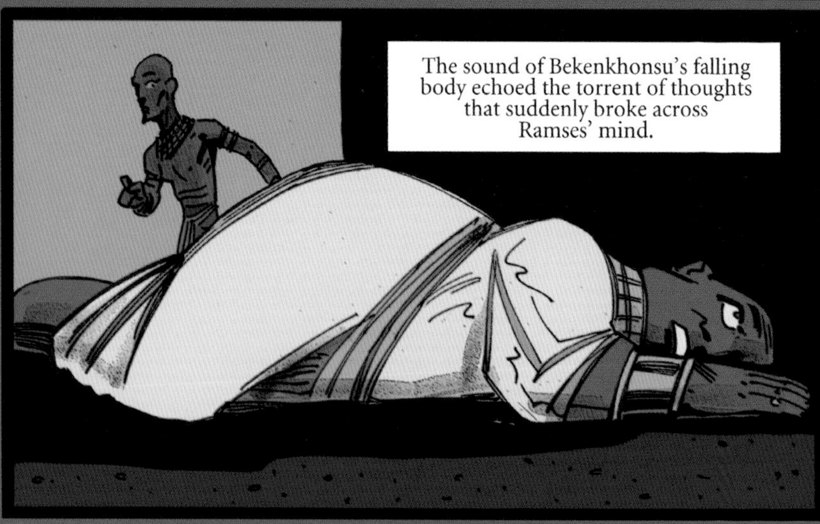

The sound of Bekenkhonsu's falling body echoed the torrent of thoughts that suddenly broke across Ramses' mind.

No mortal hand had touched the High Priest. Yet, even at a passing glance, Ramses could see that his boyhood mentor was dead.

There was something Ramses continued to value.

To cherish.
...KHEPSESHEF...
...SETI...?

There is still much left to suffer.

No blood had marked the Egyptian doorways.

Beneath the granite eyes of his Father, Ramses learned the final lesson of Yahweh.

...NO...

There is *always* something left to lose.

NOOOOOOOOOOOOOO

No scribe of Israel or Egypt wrote of the funeral procession that took place that night.

"THEIR DEAD. EVERY *FIRST-BORN,* MOSES. EVERY ONE."
Both Moses and Aaron knew that a total of ten plagues would befall the Egyptians-- Penance for generations of slavery.
They did not know, though, the full anguish it would bring.

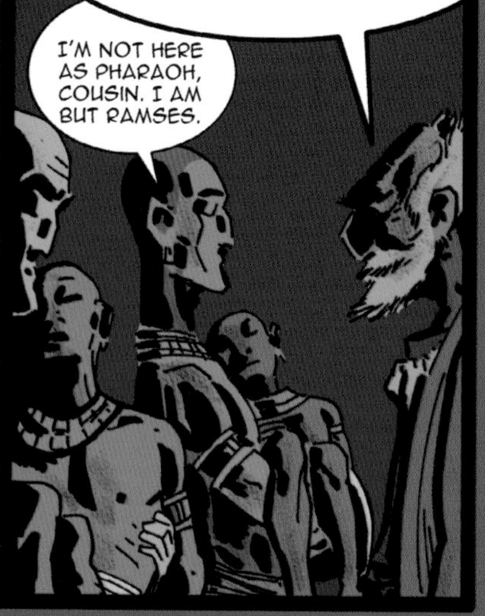
I SAID THAT THE PHARAOH WOULD NOT SEE MY FACE AGAIN. HE REPLIED THAT, ON SEEING ME, I WOULD BE STRUCK DEAD.
I'M NOT HERE AS PHARAOH, COUSIN. I AM BUT RAMSES.

I...SAW THIS END, THOUGH I DID NOT WISH IT.
I, TOO. I SAW NEITHER LEADER HOLDING AN ADVANTAGE NOR A VICTORY.
AS YOU SAID, WE ARE NOT LEADERS NOW--

"--NEITHER PHARAOH NOR PROPHET--WE ARE MEN. MOURNERS. WE HOLD ONLY OUR HEARTS."

"THEY DEPART! OFF TO BURY THEIR DEAD... HAS OUR FIGHT REACHED ITS CONCLUSION?"

"LIKELY NOT, BROTHER. NOTHING EVER ENDS, AARON."

"THE PEOPLE OF ABRAHAM NOW LEAVE EGYPT."

--REPORTS OF A STRANGE ISRAELITE ROUTE, VIZIER TA. TOWARDS SUCCOTH, BUT CAMPING IN ETHAM, THEN MOVING PAST MIGDOL.
PERHAPS THEY AVOID THE PHILISTINE WAR-FRONT.
ER. SPEAKING OF WHICH--
THE HITTITE AMBASSADOR IS HERE. YES, I SEE.
THOUGH I HARDLY RECOGNIZE THE LAND ANYMORE, VIZIER TA.
OUR GODS HAVE NOT BEEN SMILING UPON US, ANNITAS.
PERHAPS BECAUSE YOUR WAR-GODS HAVE LAIN SLEEPING TOO LONG, DESPITE *OUR* REQUESTS FOR HELP.
TELL YOUR PHARAOH THAT IT IS TIME TO UPHOLD HIS TREATY WITH MY PEOPLE.
WE EXPECT YOUR FORCES TO ARRIVE IMMEDIATELY IN OUR SUPPORT.
"BLEED WITH US IN THE SAND," VIZIER TA.

"RAMSES."
RAMSES, I CANNOT UNDERTAKE THIS DECISION IN YOUR NAME.
OUR ISRAELITES WANDER HAPHAZARDLY.
THEY MAY WELL BE CAPTURED BY THE PHILISTINES FOR USE AGAINST US...
...OR BE REPELLED BACK HERE.

MEANWHILE, THE HITTITES ARE DEMANDING OUR SUPPORT FOR THEIR OWN DEFENSE AS ENEMIES BEAT AT THEIR BORDER.
WHAT WOULD YOU HAVE US DO, PHARAOH?

THERE IS NOTHING LEFT, TA.
NO PATH LEFT TO CHOOSE.

THERE IS THE KINGDOM, SIRE--*EGYPT!*
GREAT DAYS STILL LIE AHEAD!

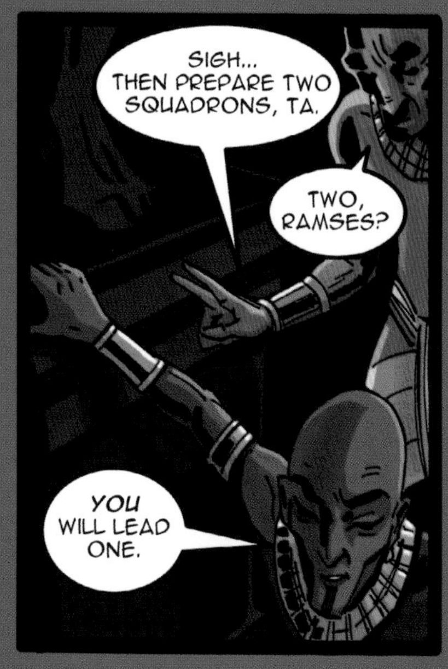

SIGH... THEN PREPARE TWO SQUADRONS, TA.
TWO, RAMSES?
YOU WILL LEAD ONE.

WE WILL GO TO PI-HAHIROTH, PAST MIGDOL.
I INTEND TO TAKE ONE SQUADRON FURTHER ON TO THE SHORES OF THE HITTITE LAND.
WHILE YOUR FORCE WILL ATTEMPT TO RECAPTURE THE ISRAELITES.
WHAT?

BUT... BUT WHY WOULD WE WANT THE ISRAELITES BACK?
WE DO NOT.
BUT WE HAVE NO OTHER CHOICE. NO OTHER PATH.

"IT IS WHAT WE ARE *SUPPOSED* TO DO."

The Israelites had not moved from their beach camp along the wide Red Sea. The mountains of Migdol loomed to their west, the land of Baal-Zephon just across the water.

The fierce wind barely stirred the thick crimson sky hanging above the shore.

"BAD OMENS, BROTHERS."

--IT IS THOUGH THE SKY BLEEDS, MOSES. IT IS NOT NATURAL.

WHO IS TO SAY WHAT IS NATURAL, MIRIAM?

WHAT MAKES A DARK SKY PROVIDED BY THE LORD LESS NATURAL THAN A BLACKSMITH'S SPEAR?

WHAT MAKES THE RARE AND UNCOMMON LESS NATURAL THAN THE MUNDANE?

"WHAT MAKES THE ANSWERED PRAYER LESS NATURAL THAN THE ORDERED COMMAND?"

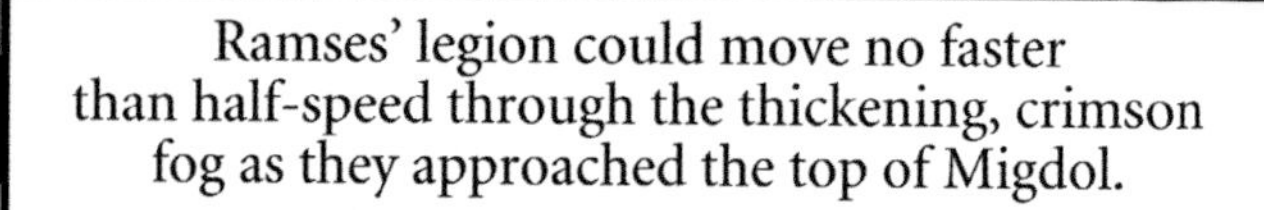
Ramses' legion could move no faster than half-speed through the thickening, crimson fog as they approached the top of Migdol.

GAH. THE LATEST PHENOMENON TO FAVOR THE HEBREWS. HAVE YOU EVER SEEN SUCH A THING?
ACTUALLY, IT REMINDS ME OF...
YOU REMEMBER THE GREAT STORMS DURING THE TENTH YEAR OF YOUR FATHER'S REIGN?

"TURNED ALL THE
GROUNDS TO A MUD
YES. WE ALL WRESTLED IN THE SLUDGE...

CHILDREN OF THE LOW CASTE AND SONS OF THE PHARAOH... CAKED IN MUD TOGETHER.
THOSE WERE GOOD DAYS. BEFORE ALL THIS DEATH.
FRIEND, THEY WERE ALL GOOD DAYS.
EVEN WITH THIS DEATH, THEY ARE ALL GOOD DAYS.

MOSES!!
THE EGYPTIANS! THEY HAVE CLEARED THE FOG-- THEY DESCEND MIGDOL!
THEN WE CONTINUE OUR EXODUS.
CHILDREN OF ABRAHAM--
--GO NOW TO THE SEA!

To her embarrassment, Rebcha had never learned how to swim.

Having lived along the Nile all her life, her enslavement never afforded her the chance to try. Nor, in truth, had her courage.
ON, FAITHFUL!

Yet now she and all the rest of the uncertain Israelites did not pause as they approached the water.

HEAR MY BROTHER! ONWARD, KINSMEN!

Instead, the sea itself seemed to hesitate at their approach, trembling and diminishing at their feet.
ONWARD!

Finally, when the tide could ebb no further--

--A new path was provided.

INCREDIBLE.
THE VERY SEA--IT FEARS TO TOUCH THEM. IT BREAKS BEFORE THEIR THRONG.

THIS...THIS FEAT IS THEIR BRIDGE TO BAAL-ZEPHON. THEY WILL THEN BE OUT OF OUR REACH.

IF WE ARE TO RETAKE THEM, RAMSES, IT MUST BE NOW!
SIRE?

PROCEED.
COMMANDERS, PREPARE YOUR MEN! BY ORDER OF THE PHARAOH, MOUNT UP FOR THE RUSH!

"GOOD-BYE, RAMSES. MY FRIEND...MY PHARAOH."

"...GOOD-BYE, TA--"

FOR THE KINGDOM!
"--MY FRIEND...MY BROTHER."

FOR THE KINGDOM!
Ta could not help but read his destiny on Ramses' face.

Still, the Vizier would not dream to avoid it. A fact which made Ramses both love his friend and be saddened for him all the more.

But there was nothing left for Ramses to do but watch and wait--

--And pray.

PHARAOH! STAND BACK!
GUARDSMAN!
W-WHOA!!!
AAAAGGGGGGHHHHHHHH!!!!

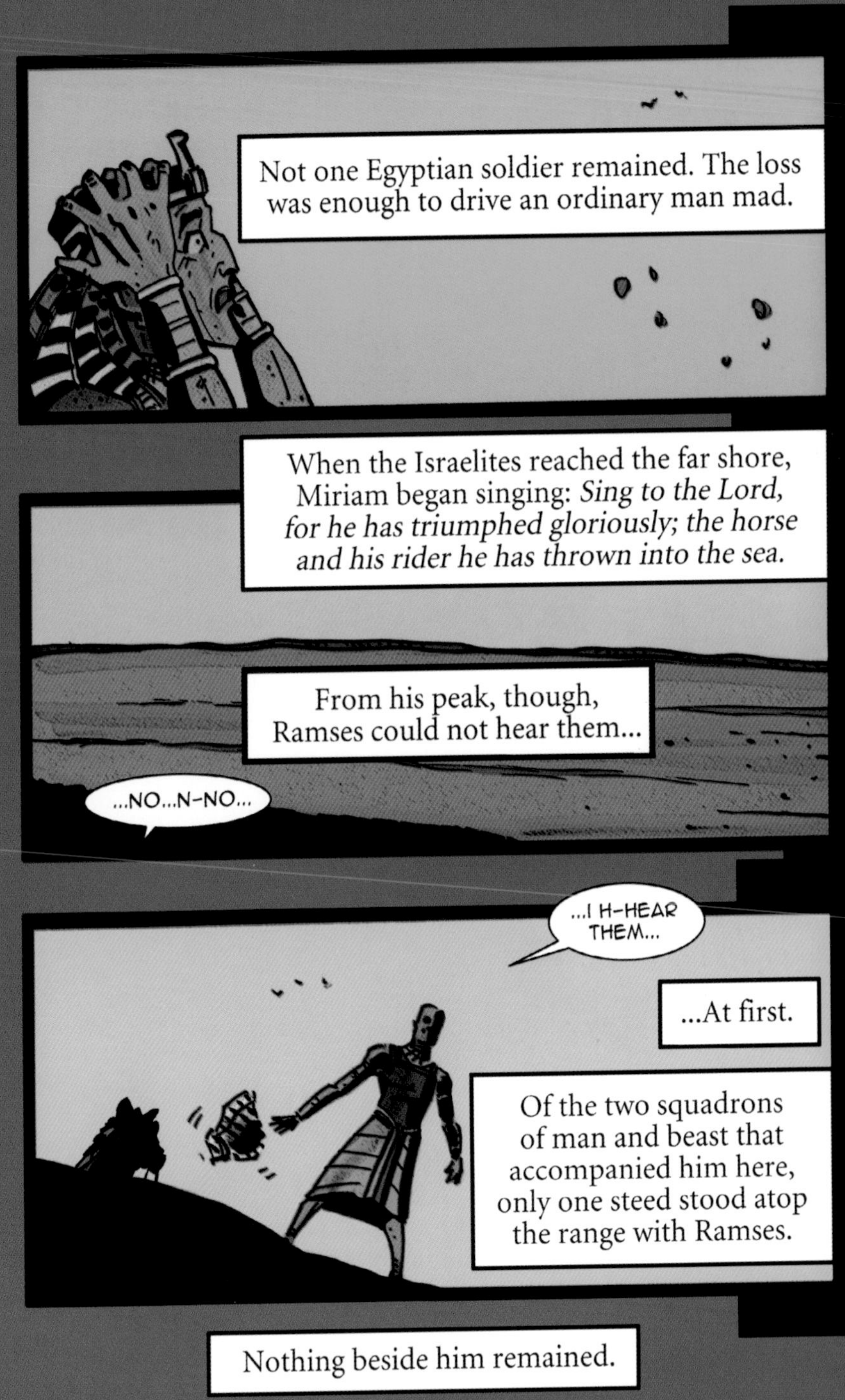
Not one Egyptian soldier remained. The loss was enough to drive an ordinary man mad.
When the Israelites reached the far shore, Miriam began singing: *Sing to the Lord, for he has triumphed gloriously; the horse and his rider he has thrown into the sea.*
From his peak, though, Ramses could not hear them...
...NO...N-NO...
...I H-HEAR THEM...
...At first.
Of the two squadrons of man and beast that accompanied him here, only one steed stood atop the range with Ramses.
Nothing beside him remained.

Like a nomad, Ramses made the long journey back to Avaris alone.

Looking decidedly common, the King of Egypt wondered whether he should indeed return to the capital.
Perhaps he was ***cursed***. Perhaps he had scorned the ***divine***.

Perhaps the woe felt by Egypt was his doing.
ENOUGH.

ENOUGGGGGGGGGGH!!

WHAT MORE WOULD YOU HAVE OF ME??
I HAVE PLAYED MY ROLE! MY LAND, MY FAMILY, MY PEOPLE-- WE HAVE PAID THE PRICE SLATED FOR US!
IS IT OVER??

WHY DO THIS?
WHAT SICK PLEASURE COMES FROM OUR SUFFERING?
REVENGE FOR THE HEBREWS?
SHEER ENTERTAINMENT?
YOU COULD HAVE FREED THEM WITHOUT HARM TO US!
YOU COULD HAVE PREVENTED THEIR ENSLAVEMENT IN THE FIRST PLACE!

DAMN YOU, WHY??
I AM MORTAL.
I NEVER THOUGHT OTHERWISE, NEVER BELIEVED THE PRIEST'S DECLARATIONS!
IF THE DIVINE TRULY CHOOSES THE HEBREWS, THEN I HAVE NO RECOURSE.
I NEVER HAVE. THEN, WHY...WHY MANIPULATE ME SO?

In answer to the Pharaoh's raging, no response came.

NO? VERY WELL. IT IS OVER NOW.
NO MORE PLAGUES WILL TORTURE MY LAND. MY PEOPLE WILL HEAL AND PROSPER.

The last of the plagues had befallen Egypt.

MY FAMILY WILL SEE PROPER BURIAL, AS WILL ALL THOSE WHO PERISHED DURING THESE DAYS.
MY LINEAGE WILL ENDURE.
AND MY KINGDOM WILL SURVIVE.
EGYPT WILL FLOURISH.

Nefertari's body was placed in the temple dedicated in her name at Abu Simbel. Khepseshef and Seti were entombed in the Valley of the Kings on the West Bank at Luxor. Ramses wife Istnofret was named Queen and bore Ramses' successor as Pharaoh: His thirteenth son, Merneptah.

I SHALL NOT DEPART THIS WORLD UNTIL EGYPT IS AGAIN MAJESTIC-- UNTIL WE HAVE TRULY OVERCOME THIS TIME OF TRIAL AND FAITH.

Ramses the Great ruled for 67 years, outlived twelve of his sons, and ordered the construction of more monuments than any other Pharaoh in history.

Many of these structures from his 19th dynasty of the New Kingdom exist to the modern day in Egypt. It is the sixteenth most-populous country in the world at 74 million people.

Merneptah named his own son Seti II, in honor of both the grandfather and nephew he never knew.

AND--
...NO.

ENOUGH.

WE ARE DONE.

FIN

AFTERWORD

When I first approached Dave Lewis about finding a project to collaborate on, I had in mind a short story, maybe something for his excellent ***Mortal Coils*** series.

Apparently, what I laughingly call a style wasn't quite right for that. But Dave saw something in my work and offered me several other projects he'd been kicking around.

One had particular appeal, the biblical Pharaoh of Moses and the Exodus story. I envisioned a tightly written scene as Pharaoh, alone with his dead eldest son, recognized through his grief that this alien Yahweh of the Hebrew slaves had been manipulating him. Every time he offered to concede freedom to Moses' people, something would harden his heart and he'd issue a retraction. Then he'd take a miraculous beating and the cycle would start over.

It was as though a bully were holding his fist and punching him with it, "Stop hitting yourself! Stop hitting yourself!" It was intolerable, and as the scene would end, the Pharaoh would refuse to tolerate it. He would stop the fleeing Hebrews once and for all, before they reached the end of his lands at the Red Sea.

That's what I envisioned.

What Dave wrote was an epic writ on a human scale, the tale of a man who tried to rule justly, love his family well, and deal with impossible demands. What a pleasure to draw it!

~mpMann

Preliminary Sketches for Moses and Aaron

Preliminary Sketches for Ramses and the Egyptians

ABOUT THE AUTHORS

THE WRITER

Emerging from the field of comic book academia, A. David Lewis has presented articles on comic book medium at conferences across the country as well as in *The International Journal of Comic Art*, The Pulse, Newsarama, and Broken Frontier, to name a few. He has edited and written for a number of small press companies including Sky Dog Comics with *Even More Fund Comics* and Silent Devil Productions with *Dracula Vs. King Arthur.* In 2002, Lewis debuted his own title, the dark suspense anthology *Mortal Coils*, which went on to be named a winner in the 2003 *Cinescape* Literary Genre Competition. The first collected *Mortal Coils* trade paperback, *Bodylines*, was released in 2004 through his Caption Box imprint, with a follow-up edition produced for 2005's Free Comic Book Day. He currently resides in Boston, MA and serves as a lecturer for the English Department at Northeastern University.

THE ILLUSTRATOR

Marvin Perry Mann began his comics career in 1989 inking *The Trouble With Girls* for Malibu Graphics, going on to illustrate *Ape City*, *Flesh Gordon* and the hilarious *Girls* spin-off *Lizard Lady*. Returning to comics in 2002, he utilized 3dsmax animation and modeling software to create a 240-page silent comic strip and two related flipbook animations for Mark Stephen Meadows' book *Pause and Effect: The Art of Interactive Narrative*. His most recent projects include *The Girly Comic*, *Smut Peddler*, *The Tethered*, and *Arcana Jayne: Hair of the Dog* with Lisa Renee Jonte.

THE COLORIST

Jennifer Rodgers is an illustrator with a Bachelor's Degree in Illustration from Moore College of Art & Design. Winner of the *Norman Cohn Award for Excellence in Applied Illustration* in 2003, she has done coloring work for Sky Dog Comics, trading card illustrations for the *Wars* Trading Card Game from Decipher, and illustrations and design work for role-playing games from Anvilwerks, Blue Devil Games, and Hero Games.